THE OTHER

ROBBIE DORMAN

The Other by Robbie Dorman

www.robbiedorman.com

ISBN-13: 978-1-958768-01-3

Cover design by Bukovero

For Kim, forever and always.

1

Bev's heart was filled with love.

Friends and loved ones surrounded them and packed their house and backyard, talking, drinking, and enjoying each other's company.

It was their 40th wedding anniversary.

Now where was Don?

She'd lost track of him at some point, waylaid by an old colleague who wanted her opinion on a new debate about canon in Modernist literature. She'd find him, she was sure. He was probably in the kitchen, camped out next to the snacks.

"Beverly!" yelled a voice, and Bev turned to see Patricia Newsted, one of her and Don's oldest friends. Patty was always fashionably late, and today was no different.

"Patty!" said Bev, going in for a hug. She embraced her warmly. Patty was twice as large as her, taller and wider, and Bev appreciated her hugs. You could always tell she meant them.

"Happy anniversary," said Patty. They talked in the den, empty except for them. The house buzzed with activity, and as they stood there, a few people walked by on their way to get another drink.

"Thank you," said Bev.

"Your present is in the car," said Patty. "Don't let me forget it."

"Oh, you didn't have to get us anything," said Bev.

"Oh please," said Patty. "How often does someone get to celebrate 40 years of marriage? I couldn't even manage five. And it's more of a present for you, than for Don. I don't think he would mind."

"He would let all the presents be for me, if he could," said Bev. "Less work for him."

Patty laughed. "Where is he, anyway? I need to give him his hug."

"I don't know," said Bev. "I was just looking for him."

"Well, I'll help," said Patty. "I'll swing through the backyard, say some hellos, and keep an eye out. Let me know if you see him."

Bev winked. "Will do."

Patty smiled again and was gone with a pat on the arm.

Bev headed into the kitchen, where a small group congregated around the snack table, and another near the drinks. They had cleared as much space as possible, but still, every inch was occupied. Bev grabbed a piece of cheese from the tray and ate it, relishing the taste.

"Happy anniversary, Aunt Bev," said Tom Milone, who left the younger group that congregated near the drink table to come to her. He hugged her tight, and she returned it. Tom was over six feet tall and well over two hundred pounds, and he engulfed her in the hug. He played linebacker for the college team. She had been there when he was born, and now he dwarfed her. He was one of the slew of colleague's children that called her Aunt Bev. Don was Uncle Don. They didn't have children of their own.

"Thank you, Tom," she said. "How are you?"

"I'm alright," he said, smiling. "Looking forward to this season."

"Team's going to compete this year?" asked Bev. She only loosely followed the team. They had historically been very, very bad.

"I think so," said Tom. "We did okay last year, and we've only gotten better over the summer. Think I can get you and Don to come to a game this season?"

"I don't know—"

"Come ooon, just one game," said Tom. "I'll make sure it's one we'll definitely win. Pleeease?"

"Okay," said Bev. "Just make sure to remind me. My memory isn't what it once was." It was what she told everyone, but her memory wasn't bad, especially considering her age. Most 68-year-olds weren't as sharp as her.

"I won't let you forget," said Tom. "I can get you good seats, too. You won't have to sit on those crappy metal bleachers."

"They still have the bleachers?"

"Yeah," said Tom. "I'm hoping that if we can get a couple winning seasons in, the college will pony up to improve the stadium. I don't know how they expect people to deal with fall weather on metal bleachers, it's just absolutely brutal—"

"Bev, we were wondering if we could get a toast from Don?" asked Will Thompson, poking his head from inside. Will helped run Math Empowering Kids, the charity learning center. Don hadn't been there in quite some years, but the center still bore their name. "Everyone's been expecting it, and I think a few people have to head back home—"

"Oh, yes, of course," said Bev. "He'd be upset if he didn't get everyone. He even mentioned how he had something special planned."

"Do you know where he is?" asked Will.

"No, I was just looking for him. He's not outside?"

"Nope," said Will. "He was out there not too long ago. I lost track. I'll ask around, see where he might have gone off too."

A flare of anxiety shot inside Bev, but she dismissed it.

"I'll look upstairs," said Bev. "He might just be taking off his tie."

"Don't even know why he wears the thing," said Will, smiling. "This isn't a faculty event."

"Habits are a hard thing to break," said Bev, before leaving the kitchen, back out through the den, into the living room. He wasn't there.

"Don's about to do a toast," said Bev, to all she passed. "Best get outside if you want to be in on it."

"Wouldn't miss it for the world," said Melissa Cawthorn, who'd been a TA under Bev, years and years ago. Now she was a tenured professor herself. She got up, and the few others there followed. Bev still needed to find Don.

Don, where did you get off to? I told you not to wander,

not tonight.

She peeked her head into the dining room, but no one sat inside. She heard people filter outside, and the house itself was quiet. Maybe he *was* upstairs. Bev didn't really believe he was taking off his tie, but it was possible he'd retreated up there and had fallen asleep. Being around crowds was getting harder and harder for him. Trying to remember everyone's name, and all their details. Bev herself struggled, she couldn't imagine what it was like—

Bev climbed up, the wood creaking underneath her feet. The stairs had lasted the past 40 years, and they had hoped it would last until they both passed. They hadn't considered home renovation in their retirement funds, and they still had planned a trip to Ireland next year—

"Don?" she asked, the house quiet. No response as she reached the top of the stairs. There were two bedrooms upstairs, along with an attic and their master bath. She stuck her head into the guest bedroom, but it was empty, undisturbed.

She walked down the hall, into their bedroom, pushing through the door.

"Don—"

But it was empty, the bed unmade.

Don, where are you—

She looked out the bedroom window into the backyard. All the guests were there, talking amongst themselves, people walking around the small area. Patty looked up with a look of confusion and threw her hands up in a shrug.

Bev went to the other side of the bedroom and looked out front. Both cars were still in the driveway, penned in by dozens of other vehicles, parked behind them and on the street. He had walked, wherever it was.

Bev rushed downstairs, her heart beating harder now, the pit of anxiety in her stomach that she had tried to deny for fifteen minutes now desperately aching. The lump of sour cold in her guts sat there, the worst things going through her mind. She hadn't thought he was this bad.

She moved through the house and into the backyard, where everyone stared at her. Patty came up to her.

"Nothing?"

"No," said Bev. "He's not inside. His car is still in the driveway."

"Mary said she saw him leave out the back path half an hour ago," said Patty.

"I didn't think much of it," said Mary, stepping up. "Thought he was taking a break from everyone."

"Maybe he went for a walk, and lost track of time," said Patty.

"Maybe," said Bev. "I'm going to look for him."

"I'm sure he'll turn up if we wait just a few minutes," said Mary.

"I'm not," said Bev, and walked past them through the small back gate that led to the path to the woods behind their house. Their neighborhood was the furthest in the city limits, their property butting up against the woods that extended out into the county. The woods were dark and big, and the narrow path led out of their backyard, through a small clearing, and into the trees. Bev hoped Don had stayed on the path. If he wandered into the forest—

Patty walked with Bev and grabbed her softly by the arm.

"What should we do, Bev?" asked Patty.

"I'm worried," said Bev. "I'm going to look for him. He's

been—foggy—lately. Would you get everyone together and have them follow behind?"

Patty met her eyes, fear now in them, and nodded. Bev turned and went out the back gate, down the path. She marched as fast as she could and the cool evening air dried the sweat that formed on her arms. She wore slim pants and sensible flats with her dark blouse, so the beaten path wasn't tricky to walk. It'd be harder the deeper she went.

Please, Don, please have stayed close.

Bev pushed past the treeline, and soon the relatively bright early evening sky was dim, and her eyes struggled to adjust as she walked. Don had been wearing his gray suit and would be easy to spot against the dark trees.

"Don?" she asked, not quite yelling. She repeated herself every five minutes as she strode, and she heard Patty and the rest of the guests behind her yell in earnest. Bev pushed ahead of them, pushed because time might be of the essence. She'd let them fan out, and explore the space around the path more completely. Bev was more worried about what laid at the end.

The cliff.

The path was actually at a slight incline, leading up through the trees. You would barely notice it until pointed out, or after walking for ten minutes and you found yourself huffing from the climb.

But the path itself was beaten, a simple walk, and it ended at the cliff that overlooked the woods proper.

The cliff overlooked the forest floor, and in the brightness of the day, the sun would pierce through the canopy. They had put a bench there to sit and enjoy the view. Together, or apart, they would come, and rest, and take in the beauty. They didn't own this land, or the view, but it some-times felt like it.

In their thirty years in the house, neither of them had ever gone past the cliff. It was a steep drop, at least forty feet if not more, with jagged rocks and snarled branches all the way down. The forest floor lay far below.

Images of Don sprawled on the ground, falling, or jumping off the cliff rolled through her mind.

You should have taken him to the doctor, you shouldn't have ignored it, and hoped it went away.

Bev pushed the thoughts away. They wouldn't help her now. She walked as fast as she could, the guests shouting behind her, their yells echoing through the forest. If Don was out here, he would hear someone. She only hoped he wasn't at the bottom of the cliff.

The path was less than a mile, snaking subtly through the trees, and her eyes were glued ahead of her, looking for Don, darting back and forth, searching for her husband, who she could identify by smell, or sound, or sight. The end of the path was approaching soon, and *please, Don, please be alright, I can't lose you yet, we had more time—*

Then she saw him.

Oh no.

He was easy to spot, silhouetted against the darkening evening sky. Don stood on the edge of the cliff, his back to her. The bench was behind him.

No, Don, no

She slowed. She didn't want to startle him.

"Don?" she asked, her voice soft, its most pleasant. He didn't answer, didn't move.

"Don? It's Bev," she said. "It's your wife, Bev. You there,

honey?"

"Hnh?" he said, a noise of confusion.

Bev heard footsteps behind her, but she didn't look back, her eyes locked on Don. She put up a hand, a single finger, trying to warn them. Bev didn't want to scare or alarm him. She wanted him to remember her, and she wanted to pull him back.

"It's Bev," she said. "It's time for the toast, at our party. Everyone's missing you."

"Bev?" he asked, his voice coming to the surface. "Bev?" he repeated.

She crept closer now, almost within reach. His toes tiptoed at the edge of the rock that fell forty feet below.

"Yes, honey," she said. "Come back over here."

"I—" she snaked a hand out and grabbed his belt, pulling him back from the cliff's edge with all her strength. Bev had never been strong. She was strong enough today, and pulled him back a few feet, and he stumbled slightly, only toward her. He turned and caught her eyes, staring at her in confusion.

"Bev?" he asked. "Where am I?"

"You're safe," she said. "You're with me."

"How did I get here?" he asked.

"You walked," she said. She glanced back. A dozen guests waited for them, all of them visibly relieved. "Let's go back home, okay?"

"Okay," he said. "Okay." He looked at her again. "I wasn't alone."

"What?"

"I wasn't alone," he said. "The Other was here. He made me come here. He wanted me to jump."

2

Bev sat in the doctor's office. It was relatively small, with the wall behind his desk covered in plaques and degrees, after years in the field of—

Dementia. Say it, Bev. He's a specialist in dementia.

They had been to five doctors before him, going from their general care doctor to a neurologist to a geriatrician to a geriatric psychiatrist and now to Dr. Baumann, who specialized in aging and memory care. They'd gone through MRIs and PET scans and test after test, putting Don through the ringer. Bev felt deeply tired, with a dark pit of worry and sorrow in her stomach. It was bad. They wouldn't have sent them to that many doctors unless it was bad.

The doctor had a thick folder in front of him, and he flipped through it, but he wasn't really looking at it, keeping his hands busy. Or maybe just searching for a specific fact before he talked to her. Bev wished he would just talk, and tell her, and let them get out of here. But Don wasn't with her, been told to stay in the waiting room, and that only concerned her more.

"Beverly," he said, and her eyes darted to him. The doctor was middle-aged, with gray hair brushed to the side to hide his balding. He wore a doctor's coat over a blue button-down shirt. His eyes were soft. "You're probably wondering why I'm only talking to you."

"Considering we're here for Don, yes," she said. "I've been interviewed multiple times—"

"I know," he said. "It can be very trying. Please be patient with me. A part of it is I need to verify what's in the notes. Another is hearing it in your own words, not some short hand version. So you may repeat yourself, and I know it can be hard. But I promise, I won't be referring you to anyone else. I'll be the one helping you and Don."

"Okay," she said, the ache still there, and she took a deep breath and tried to exhale, tried to push out some of that worry.

"When did you first notice memory problems from Don?" asked Dr. Baumann.

"He's never had a good memory, and we've been married for 40 years," said Bev.

"There's a difference between—"

"I know," said Bev. "I know. But it's what I told myself, when it really started. He forgot stuff all the time our whole lives. He'd lose his keys, or his sunglasses, even when they were right in front of his face. I always had to remind him of directions. Our whole lives. A few years ago, he forgot our anniversary."

"That was the first time you noticed?"

"Yes," said Bev. "As forgetful as he was, he never forgot dates. He was the one between us who remembered birthdays, and wedding anniversaries, and everything else. He never forgot. He always had something special for our anniversary, even on the boring numbers."

"How many years ago was it?"

"It was four years ago," she said. "And maybe I should have brought him then. But it's simple to overlook. Because everyone's memory fades as they get older. Mine certainly has. So it's easy to explain away. But he just forgot entirely. I was surprised, but it wasn't a big deal. We still went out for a nice dinner, but it didn't hurt my feelings. We've been together for so long, a lot of those things don't matter anymore. But that was the start."

"How long before it got worse?"

"Well, after that, I noticed it more. And I wasn't sure if it was happening more, and I was just noticing it, but it was least a few times a week, where he'd forget it was trash day, or he'd write the wrong year on checks, or—I don't know. Details like that. And because it was small things, I didn't think much of it."

"It usually starts out that way," said the doctor. "They're largely inconsequential."

"Yes," said Bev. "But I knew inside that it was something. I hoped it wasn't. Don's older than me by a handful of years, and I had always dreaded something like this. I wanted to stick my head in the sand."

"How long has he been wandering away?" Bev stared at the doctor and forced herself not to cry. She took another deep breath.

"Not long," said Bev. "Less than a year. His memory was getting worse and worse, but he could still function. And he knew it, so he leaned on me more. I was okay with that. Anything for Don. That's what marriage is. When one of you falters, the other picks up the slack. And so that's what I did. He couldn't remember things all the time, so I helped him. I reminded him, no matter how many times it took. He was there when it mattered, you know? When pressed, he could do it. I don't know how. Maybe he just faked it, you know. Pretended to know what he was doing. He just improvised. He had to do it for his classes for decades. But one day we were at the grocery store together—we always shopped together, we both liked to cook, and wanted a say in what we kept in the house—he had to always feel the produce, and make sure it was up to his standard. But we were at the store, and he went off to get limes, and then I went to look for him, and he was gone. I scoured the whole store, and even went to the intercom, so they could page him, but he didn't show up."

"What did you do?"

"I left my cart and left the store. I knew—" She stopped, grabbing a tissue from the box on the doctor's desk. She wiped the tears forming. "I knew what had happened. The fear had always been there. But I just ignored it. Ignored it and ignored it and ignored it."

"Where had he gone?"

"Not far, luckily," said Bev, a sad smile on her face. "Only down the plaza. There was a stationary store down there, and he was standing in front of the window, just staring at the shapes."

"What did you do?"

"I tried to be nice," said Bev. "I was so upset, so afraid, but I knew getting angry wouldn't help anything. I reminded him where he was, and what we'd been doing, and we went back to the store. But that was the last time I let him out of my sight. Until the party."

"Not once?" asked the doctor.

"We went everywhere together after that," said Bev. "I couldn't trust him not to wander away. In the house, I didn't always stay with him. I couldn't. But anytime we left, I kept a close eye on him."

"But you lost track of him at the party? Which party was this?"

"Our 40th wedding anniversary. It wasn't my idea. Several of our friends talked us into it, and it was hard for me to turn them down. It would be good for us. And I hoped it would bring back good memories for Don. Seeing all our old friends like that. Maybe he'd get a little boost from it, you know? And I figured I could leave him alone for a bit. There were tons of people there. They'd be able to keep an eye on him, surely. But he wandered off. Out into the woods behind our house."

"And you found him on the edge of a cliff?" asked the doctor.

"Yes," said Bev, and she felt the tears pour down her cheeks again. She pulled another tissue. "I'm sorry."

"It's perfectly okay."

"That's where I found him," said Bev. "I pulled him away. Got him home, along with all the guests. That was it, for the party. Most people left. Our friend Patty stayed the night, to help me. And we made appointments for the doctors."

The doctor nodded. "This probably doesn't come as a shock to you, Beverly, but Don has Alzheimer's disease. Either in stage four or five, depending on the day and his symptoms."

"How many stages are there?"

"Seven," said the doctor. "The latter stages require more and more care, as the patient's cognitive decline becomes severe. They are unable to feed themselves, or take care of basic needs. It's not linear, however. Don may have good days, where he remembers more, and bad days, where he may not seem himself at all."

Bev nodded. The ache in her stomach had lessened somewhat, even if the sorrow was still there.

"How much time until he gets worse, Doctor? Until those later stages?"

"I don't know," said Doctor Baumann. "It's hard to predict. We usually just monitor each patient's decline, and adjust as necessary. But I do want to be clear, as painful as it can be, this *will* be a decline. There is no reversing Alzheimer's. There's a lot of research, but we're not close to a cure. It's largely about managing symptoms."

Bev nodded, wiping her eyes again. "Why is Don not here with me?"

"Because in cases with couples, I like to break the news separately. In some instances, the patient isn't fully aware of what the diagnosis means. And there may be questions you have that you don't want Don to hear."

"Like what?"

"Like if an assisted living facility is the best choice. We have a good one in the area, with accredited caregivers—"

"No," said Bev. "I don't want him to be alone with strangers. We're both retired. I can handle taking care of him."

"Okay," said the doctor, nodding. "But if at any point it becomes too much, please tell me. As Don declines, his behavior might become erratic, and even though he has no history of violence—"

"Don would never hurt me," said Bev. "He's one of the gentlest people I've ever known."

"I know you're telling the truth," said the doctor. "But he may not stay himself, as he loses more function. And you need to be prepared for that. I honestly suggest visiting Dr. Allou by yourself, for some sessions. It can help you in taking care of Don, as well."

"I'll keep that in mind," said Bev. "But I don't want to give up Don to some facility, even if they do good work."

"I know you don't," said the doctor. "But in situations like this, typically your hand is forced, when aberrant behavior becomes too difficult to control. Have you seen anything like that from him?"

"I mean, not really," said Bev. "It's largely memory issues. Although—"

"What was it?"

"When I pulled him back from the cliff," said Bev. "He told me something. He told me that there was someone else there. Another person. That it wanted him to jump."

"Hmm," said the doctor, looking at her and then jotting down some notes. "Did he name them?"

"No," said Bev. "He just called him The Other."

"Sometimes patients will imagine things," said Dr. Baumann. "Situations, or people. That might be what that is. But I wouldn't be too concerned, as long as you're able to monitor him, and keep him from wandering into dangerous situations. If he mentions this other again, note it down, and tell me the next time we meet."

"Will do," said Bev.

"Are you ready to bring Don in?" asked Dr. Baumann. "We can talk about it together."

"As ready as I'll ever be," said Bev. "I'll do what I have to. I always have."

3

Bev and Don took his diagnosis and tried their best to live their life. The diagnosis hadn't surprised Don. He lived with it all the time, even if he wasn't always as sharp as he once was. But he'd been there for all of it, as his mind slowly wore away.

They tried to live their normal life. They stayed to their usual routines. Lunch and dinner out once a week. Jeopardy and Wheel of Fortune every night. They would watch the Red Sox games together and cheer whenever the Sox would do well. This season it was a little further and farther between, but they tried.

Bev did her best to maintain a normal quality of life for both of them. When Don would forget something, or wander around the house aimlessly, or start a chore and lose track of what he was doing, she would step in. She would remind him, softly, kindly. She would ask him, over and over again, even if the asking was only to soothe him.

It was a burden, yes, and she would feel it at the end of the day, when her eyes hung heavy, and she found herself brewing a second pot of coffee in the afternoon, so she could make it to the evening without falling asleep.

Because she couldn't afford naps. Any time asleep was time she wasn't watching Don. And maybe it wouldn't matter. Maybe Don would putter around the house and not harm himself accidentally. But she couldn't take the risk anymore, not after the cliff. Because all she pictured was him silhouetted against the darkening sky, ready to plummet forty feet, bouncing off jagged rocks, dead at the bottom, all because she couldn't stay awake.

So a second pot of coffee it was. She had born her share of the marriage for this long, and she would continue to do so, even if it grew bigger by the day, as Don lost more and more of himself.

They watched Jeopardy, and Don would be lucky to answer a single question. He would guess, but he couldn't keep up with the pace of the various guest hosts. She sat next to him, and held his hand, and tried to pretend nothing was wrong while Don got question after question wrong, or even worse, settled into silence as she felt a great sadness fall onto him.

But that wasn't the worst of it. The sorrow, the confusion—she could handle it. It was expected. But the anger, the darkness, the *meanness*, she hadn't expected. She hadn't lied when she told Dr. Baumann that Don was the gentlest man she'd ever met. He was soft and easy, one of the reasons she fell in love with him.

And largely, he was the same. But then there were moments when he blew up, an unseen anger rising from nowhere and lashing out at her.

They had eaten dinner, pasta and artichokes that she had cooked with a little help from Don. And Don had stopped her from washing the dishes.

"I'll take it tonight, darling," he said. The word had warmed her heart. Darling. It was his pet name for her, said without a hint of irony or snark. He meant it, every time, no matter how many times he had said it. As his memory waxed and waned, the word had disappeared from his vocabulary, and it left a hollow spot inside when he said her name, when she was so accustomed to darling. But he used it, and she smiled, a full and cherished smile that she couldn't stop. He left her with a kiss, with both their plates from the dining room table, to the kitchen, to clean up after her cooking.

But she followed him into the kitchen. She had made a habit of never leaving him alone. Bev pictured him at the cliff side, and knew it only took a moment for him to slip away.

However, she trailed him tonight only to be with him. If he would call her darling, it was a good night. He was himself, able to touch the part of his mind that felt that love for her, and she wanted as much of that time as she could get. If it was measured in minutes, or moments, she would take it, while it was still here.

He was at the sink, cleaning, as she followed him in.

"Couldn't stay away, huh?" he asked.

"Of course not," she said, coming in from behind him in

an embrace.

"I've still got it," he said, with a chuckle, and she laughed with him, squeezing him tighter. She let go and moved to the pot of remaining pasta on the stove, going to put it in the tupperware.

It felt like old times. If only for a moment. His voice reached over her shoulder.

"We will never have this again," he said, Don's tone low.

"What?" she asked. A cold arrow entered her heart.

"This is the end of this," he said, all the tone and humor that was just present in his voice now gone, devoid of any love, or charm, or kindness.

"The end of what?" she asked, the cold dart sitting there, inside her, and she only wanted to dispel it.

"The end of our love," he said. He snarled into a dark laughter. "Forty years of marriage, of love and sacrifice, of washing dishes, and it will all be gone because of some rotten flesh inside my skull. Maybe I should jump off the cliff. It will save us all some trouble."

"Don, no," she muttered, all the volume she could manage.

"You can push me if you wish," he said, his voice cutting, and she turned to look at him, because that wasn't Don, it couldn't be.

He still washed dishes, bent over the sink, but his shoulders didn't look natural, hulking, a posture she'd never seen Don take.

"Don't say things like that," she said, wanting to see his eyes, trying to get around him, to look at him.

"It is only the truth," he said. "It is merely the end we wait for. It is a matter of time. What can I do, in that time?"

Bev circled him, and put a hand on his shoulder, and turned him, to face her, so she could see his eyes. And she had taken his statement as fatalistic, as nihilistic. But then she saw his eyes, and it wasn't Don, not anymore.

It was The Other.

And those statements weren't out of sadness, or sorrow. It was an agent of chaos. Would could he achieve in that time? What pain could he cause?

"Don?"

"Don?" he asked, staring at her. There was no confusion in his eyes this time. He smiled. "Yes, Don. I'm right here."

"You're not—"

"I'm not what," he said, a veil of shadow sliding off his eyes. Whatever had taken control of him was gone, and it was just Don. Bev saw the same kindness she had known for decades in his eyes again.

"Are you okay?" she asked.

"I think so," he said. "I was doing the dishes."

"You were," she said. "But then you started talking."

"I felt someone," he said. "For a second. The other person. What did I say?"

Bev stared into his soft eyes. "It doesn't matter. Do you want help?"

"No, I can handle it," he said. "You go relax." He turned and cleaned, working quietly. Bev thought of hugging him from behind, but she stopped herself. She remembered the darkness of The Other. She couldn't bring herself to test fate again.

She retreated instead to the living room, still listening to him. Listening to make sure he wouldn't go out the back door, into the yard and into the woods, to the cliff, to dash himself against the rocks.

And as they tried to live their normal lives, Bev tested every word that Don said, to see if it was him or not. And sometimes not even his words, but his posture, as he did one chore or another. As he went to trim branches on their trees, or mow the lawn. She watched his shoulders, his stride.

And she noticed it change, from time to time. She saw the same darkness enter his eyes, as he would peer at her through a window, or from a room over. And each time that same cold arrow entered her heart, and she felt someone else in her home. It wasn't Don, and she didn't know what to do. A stranger in her home, one she didn't recognize, wearing the skin of her husband.

He lurked around her one day as she organized the kitchen.

"What do you need, Don?" she asked. Maybe he just wanted a sandwich. He always said her sandwiches tasted better than his.

But he said nothing, and she felt ice inside, her heart and lungs frozen.

"Don?" she asked, the knife block in front of her, and she grabbed a steak knife, palming it, feeling the other person behind her. She squeezed it tight in her grip, panic inside her, furious panic, ready to defend herself against this stranger in her house.

But then he wandered away, and she turned to an empty home, and the lawnmower started. He was gone again, working.

She dropped the knife, almost throwing it away from her. She looked at the sharp blade, sharp enough to kill.

I wouldn't have used it. It was on impulse.

What is happening?

Don asked her the question, and she was thankful for it. She would have never done it herself.

"What do we do, Bev?" he asked. It was quiet, the TV off, both of them reading.

"What do you mean?" she asked, looking at him. He was staring at her, his book in his lap. It was a word search, an easy task to keep his mind busy, one he enjoyed.

"We can't continue on like this forever," he said. "Like nothing is wrong."

"I—"

"I feel okay now," he said. "I feel myself. But sometimes, Bev, sometimes that other guy is there, and it's harder and harder to deny him. And I keep losing time."

"We'll do what we have been doing," she said. "We'll both do our best."

"I don't—" he started, and then stopped, and she realized he was holding back tears. He took a breath. "I don't want you to have to do this. You shouldn't have to carry so much. I don't want to live like this. I should go—"

But he couldn't finish.

"I'm not putting you in some home, Don," she said. She got up and sat next to him, taking his hand in hers. "I won't have some stranger taking care of you. I want you here. Even if it's hard."

He paused, staring at her now. His eyes almost broke her. Terror looked out at her from inside him.

"I feel him, Bev," he said. "I can feel him taking control of me, more and more. I—I don't want to hurt you."

"He's not real," said Bev. "The doctor told me your mind made him up, to help explain your cognitive problems.

That's all he is."

"He doesn't feel imagined, Bev," he said, his eyes wavering. He squeezed her hand. "He feels real. And he's bad. Thoughts I've never thought before. They're there, and I can't stop them."

He wiped away a tear.

"I'm afraid."

4

It would be quick.

It was late at night, and Don was watching television, and Bev needed to shower. She'd been putting it off for days, not able to find a time to leave Don to himself. Layers of deodorant and dry shampoo had built up over time, and her skin crawled. She needed a shower.

They had both dozed off on the couch, a Red Sox game on, and she got Don up, and he went to bed. She was dead tired as well, exhausted even, but this was her chance. Don would be out like a light, and she could take a nice shower. It would be quick, but she'd at least be able to get clean, to wash her hair. To forget everything under the hot water, if only for fifteen minutes.

Fifteen minutes. That was plenty of time. She waited in

bed with Don, keeping herself awake, making sure he was dead asleep, his breathing soft and steady. Don had always slept like a rock, and this was her chance, just a few minutes to relax. She needed it.

She took one last glance at Don, his eyes closed, and she ducked into their bathroom, with double sinks and a big shower. They'd had it remodeled after they'd retired, having outgrown their old bathroom decades past. They had the money, and it was about time they had the one they wanted.

Double vanities, a huge shower with the regular and rainfall shower heads, and a bench. Bev had wanted a bench in the shower for ages, even just to shave her legs, but now that they were older, being able to sit for a spell was a godsend.

Bev turned the water hot, just below scorching. She'd always liked her showers blazing, her skin red when she exited, the cool air of the house soothing her. She climbed in, and the intense water immediately embraced her, and she stood underneath, letting it pelt her.

She washed, scraping off days of worry and anxiety, letting it swirl down the drain. Once she was out, she'd worry again, she'd dote again, keeping a close eye on Don, and on the worrying presence of The Other. Bev would worry about her husband becoming a different man entirely, of his personality disappearing under the oncoming wave of Alzheimer's, washing away everything familiar about him, his appearance the same but everything underneath different.

She would worry about that once she stepped out from the shower again, and left the bathroom, and would join her husband in bed. But for now, she emptied out all those terrible thoughts, of all the things she'd already experienced, of the terror of seeing Don at the cliff side, of the awful ache of the doctors, and the tests, and the diagnosis. Of the constant vigilance required to keep Don in the front of her mind, all day long, no breaks, never being able to sleep in, always having to make sure she woke up before him, that she never took a nap, never dozed off during a baseball game.

The hot water swept it all away. Bev took a deep breath, filling her lungs with the moist air, holding it for a moment, and then letting it all out. She did it again, and then again, her breath emptying her mind of everything.

The tremendous weight on her shoulders eased, and even breathing felt easier. Bev washed, rubbing away all the accumulated grime from the past few days. She rinsed, washing it away, just like the worry and the anxiety. She stood under the hot water, and it took her away.

She should leave the shower now, she should. She was clean, and ready to get out, dry off, and steel herself for her life of watching Don like a hawk.

But the water felt so good, and she stood under it, letting it beat on her, her pale skin pink, the heat of the shower in her head and face, and she didn't get out. Instead, she sat down on the bench, sitting so the water would still hit her, the cool marble relieving some of the heat. She bent over, elbows on knees, her hands on her face and in her hair, holding herself.

She cried, the tears coming without thought or provocation. The shower carried them down the drain as well. Bev silently wept, her body shaking, the pain and trauma of the past weeks and months overwhelming her, of the simple fact that the person she most needed to help her was lost inside her husband's head, his mind slowly fading away, the one she went to for support and guidance not there any-more, and even less there, day by day.

Bev cried, sitting in their ideal shower, that they had worked their whole lives for. Her tears dried up, everything washed down the drain, but she sat there still, the hot water covering her, her body pink, her face red, her soul empty.

She pushed herself up, her body complaining, her bones creaking and her joints aching, but she forced herself up, and then turned off the water, before its spell could entrance her again.

Bev didn't know how long she'd been in the shower, but it was longer than fifteen minutes. She dried off quickly, and threw on her nightclothes. The water had sapped what little energy she had left. She'd collapse into bed next to Don, and let sleep take her away.

She turned off the light in the bathroom before she opened the door. She didn't want to disturb Don. The bed-room was there, the expansive bed waiting for her, a bundle on the left side that was Don, and then her eyes adjusted, and as she was about to collapse into bed, she realized.

The bed was empty.

"Don?" she asked, her eyes maybe tricking her. Maybe he was there, and the shadows had fooled her.

"Don?" she asked again, louder this time.

But no answer, and her hands went to the blankets and sheets and ruffled through them, and the bed was empty, and Don was gone.

Oh no, oh no

She shouldn't have taken the shower, she should have waited until someone else was here, and she looked to the clock, and she had been in there an hour, how was that possible, but he could have been gone for that entire time. She threw on shoes and yelled again.

"Don!" she yelled, hoping for an answer, or at least some noise, but there was nothing. The house was empty. He was gone, had to have been, maybe he was asleep downstairs. She glanced out the bedroom window for a moment, and both their cars were still there.

Thank God he didn't drive.

But then she remembered the cliff, and the forest in the dark, and she moved downstairs, as fast as her legs would allow. All the aches and weariness had vanished now, adrenaline pumping through her body, and she grabbed a flashlight from the utility table in the kitchen.

She glanced around, but he wasn't napping in the living room, or the den, and he had to have gone to the woods, of course that's where he went, and her mind whirled.

"Please, Don, please not the cliff," she said aloud, like a magic spell, a prayer to anyone listening. She rushed outside, turning on the flashlight, the light by the back door only reaching a dozen feet from the house, the path leading off their yard the extent of its reach.

Bev looked around quickly, thinking maybe she should tell the neighbors, she could use the help, but she dismissed it, any moment lost could be the end of Don and she went out the back gate, onto the slim, worn trail that led to the forest.

"Don!" she yelled again, her voice echoing across the small field. There was no reply. She hadn't expected one.

She pushed, the flashlight's beam illuminating only the few feet ahead of her. Bev listened for anything, any noise, any sound. Don could be ten feet off the path and she wouldn't know.

He was fine, he had to be fine, everything was okay.

She repeated it inside, over and over as she moved deeper and deeper into the woods, drawing closer and closer to the cliff, dreading that she would find him there. Or even worse, finding him at the bottom.

"Don!" she yelled again, the trees catching most of her voice, and she swung the beam across the woods, hoping to catch the silhouette of Don, inexplicably in the forest, chasing something his mind couldn't know in the dark, The Other leading him to nothing.

She walked faster still, her aching bones resisting, the adrenaline wearing off, but she continued anyway. She wouldn't stop now, no matter what her body told her. It was her fault he was out here, she shouldn't have taken the shower, she shouldn't have taken her eyes off him, and then she realized she was almost to the cliff.

Her lungs froze for a moment, and Bev dragged a breath in, and forced her feet forward. She hadn't found him yet. Where else would he be, where else could he be?

The cliff lay in front of her, and she walked toward it, slowing down, her light scanning the area for Don, for the edge of the cliff. She didn't want to tumble off in the dark, bouncing off the rocks.

"Don!" she yelled again, but there was still no response, and her flashlight caught the edge of the precipice, disappearing into the darkness beyond it, and she cautiously approached, taking small steps until she stood at the brink, the darkness filling the void beyond. She stood there, her light scanning in every direction, looking for any sign of her husband.

He couldn't have, he couldn't have—

She pointed her flashlight down, looking for any sign, clothing, a dropped item, *blood—*

But there was nothing, but the light didn't reach the bottom, obscured by the various protruding rocks and branches of nearby trees. She'd have to climb down there to be sure, oh God, oh Don, but there was nowhere else he would be, and she wouldn't leave him, even if it took her all night—

A sound interrupted her from her right. A sloughing noise, both familiar and unrecognizable.

"Don!?" she yelled.

No answer, but the sloughing sound again. It was not an animal. No matter how she tried to shape it, no animal could make that noise. It was a sound made my man. Made by Don. There was no one else out here tonight. Her heart eased, if only a little. He hadn't answered her, but he was alive. And he hadn't jumped off the cliff.

She went toward the noise, off the trail. She pushed past the brush, through the piled mass of dead and rotting leaves that were on the woodland floor. Still, she heard the sound as she got closer.

Shhh-shunk. PFfffff.

Shhh-shunk. PFfffff.

Shhh-shunk. PFfffff.

It got louder, and she didn't call Don's name anymore, didn't know if she should, didn't know what he was doing, and what interrupting him would do.

But soon she was right on top of the noise, the small sound echoing off the trees, and she pushed through the last piece of brush and she saw Don, alive, standing there, and the vice grip on her heart released, and she could breathe again.

What was he doing?

He stood, turning toward her now, her light catching him in the back, and he held something in his hand.

A shovel.

And then everything clicked into place, and she recognized the sound. The sound of the shovel moving dirt. Of cutting through the earth, and dropping it down.

The sound of something being *buried.*

"Don?" she asked. He stared at her, not shielding his eyes from the light, and the look in his eyes was the same as the other day, the blank darkness, and she couldn't recognize her husband.

She moved her light off him to the pile of dirt he stood over.

He had dug a shallow pit, and was now filling it with soil. It was only half done, a mound still there next to him. Sweat soaked muck caked his face, and his dark eyes pierced through the filth.

"What are you doing?" she asked, her voice only half coming out, because she wouldn't ask this man who was not her husband his business, because he wouldn't answer.

And he didn't, only staring, the darkness in his eyes unreadable. He turned, facing her completely, moving the shovel next to him, planting its sharp, flat edge against the ground.

The anxiety of his disappearance was now replaced by something else, something else she couldn't understand, not at first, and horror joined it as she recognized it, an utter fear and terror of her own husband, the incredible love she had of him overshadowed by dread.

His gentle hands squeezed the handle of the shovel and he stared at her.

"Don!" she yelled, and she yelled again, louder. "Don!" She practically screamed, her vocal cords tense with pain.

He blinked once, twice, and the darkness left him, his fingers twitching, and then the shovel fell as he let go of it, his hands going to his face, rubbing the sweat from his eyes, covering his face with more dirt.

Bev went to him then, putting her arm around him, recognizing him again. It was Don, the man she loved, the man she had loved for decades. When his hands came away, it was him, through and through. Dirty, sweaty, confused, but him.

"Bev?" he asked. "Where am I?"

"Out in the woods," she said. "You got out of bed and came out here."

"What? Why?" he asked.

"I don't know," she said, grabbing him, wrapping an arm around him. She ushered him away from the hole, away from the shovel. Don didn't question her or resist, and they walked back to the path, and back to the house.

They left the shovel behind, and Bev helped Don, watching him, wondering if that darkness would enter his mind again. But it didn't, banished by her scream.

They got home, and cleaned up, and went to sleep, and Bev made sure Don was fully asleep before she passed out. It would be another night of brief rest, making sure she was up in the morning before him.

Up in the morning before him, to think.

To find a way to get away from him, to find out what was half buried in that hole.

5

"Are you ever serious about anything?"

Bev sat across from Don, books open between them on the table in the small courtyard outside of the Greenwood College Library. The cool air lightly blew past them, ruffling the pages of the books. He had wanted the tutoring session outside. He had said he thinks better outside, and while she thought it was foolish, it was a lovely day, so she had agreed.

They had just gotten started, and he had already derailed them multiple times with silly discussions about nothing. And this wasn't the first time. She had agreed to tutor him in his literature class because she needed help in her math classes, and they had agreed to the swap. But even when he was tutoring her, they rarely stayed on topic. It frustrated the hell out of her.

He looked at her after her comment, taken aback. She thought he was faking his reaction, but after a moment, it was clear he wasn't. He was genuinely surprised she had asked him.

"Me?" he asked. "Of course I am."

"Oh, don't act so shocked," she said. "I don't think we've even covered the bare facts of Moby Dick over three tutoring sessions. You want to talk about what movies are out, or the weather, or if I think the lit professor is a cat person or a dog person. I thought math majors were supposed to be boring."

"Boring?" he asked. "Just because we are numbers people doesn't mean we can't have personalities. I'm sorry I like things that aren't math—"

"That's not what I mean," said Bev. "I'm sorry I even brought it up—"

"No, no," said Don. "You asked me a question. I'll answer it. Yes, I am serious, from time to time. I'm serious about getting my degree. I'm serious when I vote. I would say I'm serious when I drive. But other than that, no, I'm not that serious. What are you serious about? Everything?"

"No," said Bev. "I just want us to actually get some work done."

"What? Moby Dick?" he asked.

"Well, yes," she said. "It's why we're here, isn't it?"

"I guess," he said. She eyed him, and he met her eyes before looking back down at the books, both Moby Dick and the study guide, and then his notes. And then everything clicked into place. She stared at him, her eyes narrowing slightly, her lip curling into a question.

"Is this about Moby Dick at all?"

"What?" he asked. "What do you mean?" There was something else on his face, and now he wouldn't meet her eyes.

"Don," she said. "Look at me." He looked up, a smile on his face.

"Tell me you actually needed tutoring on Moby Dick," she said.

"I need tutoring on Moby Dick," he said, smiling wide, looking at her.

"You're lying," she said.

"No," he said. "Not completely. I do need to write an essay on Moby Dick, and I certainly know nothing about that gargantuan tome, that terrible thing that weighs as much as two math books."

She studied his face. "But—"

"But I don't *necessarily* need *your* help with Moby Dick. I'm sure I could get by if I really needed to."

She sighed. "So you're wasting my time—" She sighed again, and closed Moby Dick, and the study guide, and went to put them in her bag.

"Bev, please," he said. He put his hand on the large novel. "I did not intend to waste your time. And if you need help with your math work, I will happily provide it."

She looked at him. "Why would I—" She sighed again. "Why, Don? Why?"

He met her eyes now, confusion on his face, which broke into a slight smile. "I—" He started, and then chuckled. "I thought we were on the same page."

"What page?" she asked. "What are you talking about?"

"I feel like an idiot," he said. "I'm sorry."

"Sorry about what?" she asked.

"I thought—" He took a deep breath. "I thought you were interested in me, you know? And this was a way for us to talk, to know each other, without committing to a real date. And maybe if it went okay, we'd move onto that. And sure, if we really needed it, we'd do the tutoring stuff, but I had talked to Eileen about it beforehand, and she had told me you liked me, and I thought well, I could ask you to do the tutoring swap thing, and then—"

His cheeks were reddening, and he had looked away from her now. "What did Eileen tell you?"

"She said you had expressed interest in me," he said. "So I thought this would be harmless. I guess I was wrong, or she was wrong. Or both. I'm sorry, I really am. I thought you were enjoying yourself, and kind of understood what was happening. We don't have to keep—"

"Wait," she said. "This was all to talk to me?"

"Well, yeah," he said. "I didn't know what else to do. You're so busy, and you always seem so dedicated to everything on your plate, that it was kind of imposing. I figured this was a way for us to talk and make it seem important."

"You could have just asked me out, Don," said Bev. "I'm not a lion. I won't maul you."

"I don't know," he said, meeting her eyes again. "You're kind of intimidating."

"Me? Intimidating?" she asked.

"Well, yeah," he said. "I don't mean that as an insult. Maybe I over thought everything. I just wanted to talk to you a bit. But I fucked it up. I *am* sorry."

She eyed him. Eileen couldn't have just told her that Don was interested, no, she had to tell him to use this contrived nonsense to get them together—

"I'll go," he said. "I won't waste any more of your time."

"Don—" she said. "Wait."

He looked at her, sitting back down.

"I don't think this was the best way to go about this," she said. "But—"

"Buuuut?"

She looked at him, and a smile formed on her face. She couldn't help it. His tousled hair hung over his warm eyes, and he smiled again now.

"What are you doing tonight?" she asked.

6

Don started laughing.

Bev knew the sound of his laughter. She had heard it countless times over their years together, and could recall it at will. It started softly at first, almost inaudible it was so low, but then it would explode out into an impossible to stop rollercoaster of giggles, and wheezing, and hysterics.

Don wasn't an easy one to crack, though. He smiled often, and would chuckle all the time, but it would take something special to get him to breakdown. She prided herself on being able to crack him, to make him burst into insane laughter so bad he couldn't function anymore.

It had bothered her at first, when she couldn't get him to really laugh. But then she learned what tickled his funny bone, and over the years, she had honed it down to the barest elements that always made him howl. He liked wordplay, the dumber the better. He loved Monty Python, and absurdist humor as well, but it was extremely hit or miss.

But most of all, he loved puns. The worse the pun, the harder he'd laugh. It would always knock him for a loop, and Bev waited to bring them out when he wasn't expecting it, because it would always double the intensity. She loved to hear him laugh like that, because it inevitably would result in her laughing too, as hard as him, which would make him giggle more, and they would bounce off each other, back and forth, until they were both crying, until neither could breathe.

But over time she had it down to a science, and could routinely break him once a week. It was almost a game, with Don on guard for it, waiting for her attack, and she would wait until he was completely unguarded before letting loose, and breaking him.

She loved the sound of his laughter. It was one of the things she had missed the most lately, because for whatever reason, the puns didn't work the same on him anymore. She had reserved one the other week, waiting for him, and then unleashing, right when he would least expect it.

No reaction, not even a smile. She knew he had heard it, and had recognized it, but there was nothing. Bev had thought at first that maybe it just wasn't good enough to crack him, but she knew otherwise. It was a realization, one of many that had cascaded over the months, even before the diagnosis made it official. The understanding that her husband was vanishing before her eyes.

But she still tried, over and over, having been in that same pattern of trying to make her husband laugh for four decades, and she wouldn't stop now, no matter how many times he looked at her confused.

She was in the kitchen, getting dinner ready, and Don was in the living room, watching television. It sounded like the news, but she couldn't be sure. Bev couldn't see him directly, but she could hear him and the TV, and he wouldn't be going anywhere without her realizing.

Bev made them dinner, a simple casserole tonight, but she also needed to clean out the fridge, and empty the dishwasher, and she was listening in on Don in the living room, but not completely, just enough to know if he was getting up, because she knew he could disappear in a moment if she wasn't careful, and then he started laughing.

She knew Don's laughter innately, like the back of her hand.

This was something different.

It was a dark laugh, loud, uproarious, snarling at the end of every note. And as moments passed, it only grew, getting louder and louder, filling not just the living room, but the entire house. It was a terrible cackle that echoed in Bev's ears, a sound she'd never heard from Don before, a *mean* laugh.

She walked into the living room, forcing herself to get closer to the source of that terrible noise.

"Don?" she asked, as she entered the room, her eyes going to the TV, seeing what Don was laughing at.

Misery.

He was laughing at misery.

It was the news. He'd been watching it, and Bev had tuned out the drone of the anchors talking as she cooked. A thought had entered her mind, a hope, really. A hope that

Don had turned the channel to something funny, and that this new laugh was at something innocuous. And sure, it wasn't the laugh she was used to, but Don was changing, and she was doing her best to adapt to this last stage of his life. Her love for him was complete, and she would adapt if she had to. She wouldn't take joy from him, no matter how much it hurt her.

So there was still hope in her that this laughter, which sounded awful and mean and *evil*, wasn't that, but just a different laughter, a laugh created by Don's mind rewiring itself, working through the damage created by Alzheimer's.

But this wasn't that.

He was laughing at pain. The news showed bombed-out buildings in Syria, with people being stuffed into body bags, with victims being interviewed, with children crying. People walked by the camera, covered in dust and debris, and Don's laughter grew and grew and grew.

And she knew it wasn't Don in there. It was The Other.

"Don?" she asked again. "Why are you laughing?"

He continued to laugh.

"Don! Stop!" she yelled, now, and then he turned toward her, and confirmed her belief. Don wasn't there. The laughter stopped suddenly, the terrible noise finally over.

"Why?" he asked, staring at her, his voice cold, arrogant, self-righteous. Impudent. Like a child.

"Because it is bothering me," she said. "Because you shouldn't laugh at something so horrible. Please, Don." She stared into his eyes, trying to beckon her Don back to the surface. It had worked before, her presence. Her reassurance. It had been enough. "Please." She softened her voice, the tone that soothed Don, always calmed him down when something upset him.

But those cold, hard eyes just stared right back.

"But—it's—so—fun—ny," he said, enunciating every syllable. He stared at her for a moment longer, and then turned back toward the television, and started laughing again, like hitting a switch, the laughter effortless, an impossible distinction between performance and authenticity.

A surge of rage filled Bev and she grabbed the remote and turned off the TV, turning off the misery. Don's laughter stopped, and he looked at her again, The Other looked at her again.

There was something else there in his eyes now, the nothing filled with something.

Anger. Seething anger underneath the surface, and Bev took a step back. It had been reactive, an unconscious action, because his eyes scared her. An unrecognizable terror filled her, and The Other saw it, and the anger vanished, and he smirked.

Don stood up. Don wasn't a physically imposing man, and in his old age, he was even less so. But he moved with a sureness and capability she hadn't thought possible, and he strode around the couch to her, and Bev had to force herself to hold her ground, to not run, to not flee and hide in the bathroom. He approached her quickly, the smirk still on his face, staring her in the eyes, nothing but darkness peering at her, and in a flash, he snatched the remote from her hand, and turned on the TV without breaking eye contact, the sound of misery and pain filling the living room again.

"It's. Just. So. Funny," he said, punctuating every word, and then he broke eye contact, and returned to the couch, where he had sat a moment ago, and put his legs up, and laughed again, leaving Bev there without a second glance. She stood there, afraid and angry. A tear fell down her cheek and she wiped it away. She didn't want The Other to see it, even if he hadn't even looked at her after he had gotten the remote back.

She went back to the kitchen quickly, out of the room, but the laughter followed her.

Bev waited, the casserole cooking, waiting for the laughter to stop. Her eyes were glued to the timer on the oven, hoping that she wouldn't have to feed that thing, that other personality that had taken over her husband. She wouldn't know if she'd be able.

It ticked down, second by second, and the laughter continued, and continued, and then—finally—it stopped. And she waited, she waited, and it was done. She looked back into the living room, expecting that dark thing to be there, waiting, but Don was sleeping, his head back, his eyes closed, the channel on a baseball game.

The Other was gone again, dispelled. She could breathe. But the fear of him still lingered.

*

She hadn't forgotten about the mound of dirt in the woods, and after that laughter, and The Other's persistence, she couldn't put it off. She just needed an opportunity away from Don to investigate.

Bev waited until that night, until Don fell asleep. She had doubled her coffee input that evening, and her heart raced. Exhaustion tugged at her, and she knew she would crash later, but right now she was wide awake, and she let Don fade into sleep and stay there for a solid thirty minutes, until she left the bed, sliding on shoes, and leaving the room.

She had thought it over, and she couldn't leave him with free rein of the house, all alone. Would he wake up again? She didn't know, but she couldn't risk it. Their bedroom door opened out, and she took a chair and wedged it underneath the handle. He'd have to break the door to open it.

Bev went downstairs and retrieved the shovel from where they had left it. She had the shovel, and she had a flashlight, and all she had to do was walk down the path, and into the woods, and to the spot she had pulled Don from the night before.

But her neighbor's words from that morning echoed in her mind.

She'd gone out to get the paper. Don used to do it, but like many of his daily routines, the Alzheimer's had destroyed it.

Gloria was there, at the end of her driveway, the next house over. Bev waved. She wasn't super close to Gloria, but they were friendly, and Gloria had offered any help necessary after she had heard the news about Don. Gloria walked over and asked Bev the question that now echoed in her mind.

"Hey Bev, have you seen Gus around?"

Gus was Gloria's dog, a small terrier, that yapped a fair bit but wouldn't hurt a fly. Bev had told her no, even as her heart froze.

Don had buried something out in those woods. And her Don would never hurt an animal, not unless it was life-or-death. But The Other—

Bev took a deep breath and walked down the path in the dark at a brisk pace, the light from the flashlight leading the way. She carried the shovel on her shoulder. She tried to push every thought out of her mind, because if she held them too long, she would turn back now.

Her knees and ankles were still sore from her harried walk from the night before, but she pushed through the pain, and soon neared the cliff, and now all she had to do was find the spot in the trees that Don had dug.

Bev shoved through brush, and past clusters of trees, trying to remember the exact spot—it wasn't far, she knew—maybe she got turned around, and she swung the light around, looking for a landmark to ground herself with, and then her foot slipped on the mound of remaining dirt, and she was there.

The half dug hole—

Grave

The half dug hole was still there, just as they had left it. It wasn't deep, maybe only a foot down, two feet by two feet square, almost all filled. Don had worked quickly. Or maybe he was just finishing his work from some other time, when he had slipped away without her realizing, but that was impossible—

She quieted her mind, the light focused on the hole. She held the shovel in one hand, the sharp edge planted in the ground.

What did you bury, Don?

There was only one way to find out, to unbury whatever it was, and reckon with it. She forced the shovel into the loose soil, the flashlight propped on some nearby branches, and then she paused.

Thoughts flashed in her mind, of that reckoning.

Of Don being a killer.

Of Don being taken from her.

Of Don spending his last days locked up, being watched by strangers. Given drugs, and eating crappy food. Of her new life, alone, without him, and his final moments being inside a cell.

Her heart hurt, her guts burned, and she held the shovel in two hands. She could feel sweat drip down her back. The night was silent.

She pulled the blade out of the pit, and plunged it into the small mound of dirt, and filled the rest of the hole.

7

"Thank you, Tim, for doing this," said Bev.

Tim smiled, and looked down. "It's no big deal, Bev. Just a couple hours. Give you and Patty some girl time. Give you a little bit of a break, right?"

"It's more than that," said Bev. "It's just not spending a few hours with Don—" She stopped, and took a deep breath. Don sat in the passenger seat of Tim's pickup, buckling himself in. Tim had volunteered to take Don out fishing. They'd gone fishing hundreds of times in their lives, but they had largely stopped the last couple years, mostly because of Don's condition.

"I know," said Tim. "It's fine. It may not be the same as it once was, but it'll still be nice to go out on the boat with him again."

"Just please, be careful with him," said Bev. "It's hard to explain without being around him—"

"He'll have a life jacket on at all times, and I won't let him out of my sight," said Tim. "You don't have to worry. I took care of my mother, and she had the same symptoms. We'll have a good time." He smiled, and turned to get in his truck.

"Tim—"

He turned back.

Bev thought of the dark eyes and sinister laughter of The Other. Of him swiping the remote from her.

Of the hole out in the woods.

"Nevermind," she said, smiling. "Thank you."

He nodded and got in the truck, closing the door, and pulling away. She watched Don through the windshield as they drove off. He looked normal. He looked happy, even.

But it was harder to look at him and not see those dark eyes, lurking somewhere inside.

Bev tried to push all those thoughts away. She had the rest of the day to herself and didn't have to worry about Don right now. She needed to rest and relax. This was a marathon, and she would use the time to recuperate. She'd have plenty of chances to think about Don after he came back.

*

Patty hugged her tight when she saw her at the little cafe downtown half full on the weekday.

"How you doing, Patty?" asked Bev, as they sat down, the waiter dropping off water.

"I'm fine," said Patty. "The salon is getting swamped lately. I'm trying to find another full-time hairdresser. Maybe even hiring a barber, just to work on men. There's a lot of demand for that, too. The zoomers care about how they look. Doesn't bother me at all, means more business—enough about me. Are you doing okay, Bev?"

Bev looked at her. "I'm okay," she said. "It's nice to be out with you."

"It's been a long time," said Patty. "With just the two of us."

"I would like to go out more, it's just—"

"I know," said Patty. "I don't blame you, honey. I know things have gotten bad with Don—"

"I can't leave him alone," said Bev. "Ever. It's too risky."

"Has he gotten that bad?" asked Patty. "I know he has those episodes."

"He's getting worse—" Bev tried to keep speaking, but her breath wouldn't come, and her lungs shook, and she cried, the tears coming unbid. She put her hands to her face, not wanting to make a scene, but then the tears were coming even harder, and she started to sob, with huge heaving breaths, and she couldn't stop them now. Patty stood up and ushered her outside to the cool air. Patty sat her down on a bench and held her as she cried. Her embrace was warm, and she hugged her tightly as Bev's body shook, warm tears pouring out of her.

Eventually they subsided, the unending font of pain temporarily over. Patty pulled tissues from her purse and handed them to Bev's grasping hands, and Bev wiped her face, and blew her nose.

"You feel better?" asked Patty.

"A little," said Bev. "We should tell the waiter—"

"Oh, whatever, he'll figure it out," said Patty. "You don't

have to do this alone, you know? You have a lot of friends, and they'll all help, if you need it."

"I feel bad asking for help," said Bev. "I should be able to do it alone. Thats what marriage is. Taking up the burden of your partner if they can't."

"I don't think you can directly apply that principle," said Patty. "Especially in a case like this. If you need a break, you call one of us, and we'll help."

"It's more than wanting to do it alone, Patty," said Bev. "I'm just afraid. Afraid that Don'll get hurt, and I'll resent whoever I left him with. He's with Tim today, and I trust Tim, I do, hell, he even helped his own mother with the same thing, but what if he falters for a moment, and Don gets hurt? I don't want to hate Tim. I don't want to hate any-one."

"Oh honey, you won't hate anyone," said Patty. "And nothing will happen. You worry too much—"

"And I'm not just afraid of Don getting hurt. I'm afraid of Tim getting hurt."

Patty was silent, reading Bev's face.

"Has Don hurt you?" she asked, finally. "Because if he has—"

"No," said Bev. "No, he hasn't hurt me." Her mind went to the hole in the woods.

"But—"

"But—" started Bev. "I—"

"What is it, Bev?" asked Patty. "Tell me."

Bev stared at her.

"There's someone else in there with him."

"What? What does that mean?" asked Patty.

"Don calls him The Other," said Bev. "He talks about

him like he's another person. That makes him do things. Bad things."

"Have you told the doctor about this?"

"Yes," said Bev. "He said it would seem scary, but it's something that happens. Patients with dementia sometimes have personality changes. And that's all it is. Don trying to deal with what's happening inside his mind."

"It does sound strange, but if the doctor said it's okay—"

"He scares me, Patty," said Bev. "I've never been scared of Don, ever, in my entire life. But when The Other is in there, when he's out in front, you know—the way his eyes look, the way he speaks. It's someone else. And he's mean. He's awful. I—" Bev took a deep breath. "If it was just Don I had to worry about, I could do this forever, even if Don was gone entirely. I got forty years with Don. Forty good years. I'd take care of him forever if I had to. I would gladly take that trade if offered. But The Other—I don't know if I can keep this up."

"Bev," said Patty. "I know the doctor has probably told you, but—but have you thought about having someone take care of him for you? Someone with proper training, just in case this other personality ends up being more dangerous. I'm sure there are places that are better equipped than you—"

"I won't put him in a home, Patty."

"Bev," said Patty. "If he's a danger to you—" Patty took a deep breath. "The last thing Don would want is for you to get hurt."

"I know," said Bev. "I know. And when it's The Other, that makes perfect sense. But that's not what I imagine. I imagine putting Don into one of those places, and I'd make sure it was a nicer place, with his own room, and everything, but I can only imagine when Don comes back out, when he's my Don again—" Bev felt tears push out again, and she paused, and pushed them back down. "I imagine Don coming out, in the night, not remembering anything, or even worse, remembering me, and I'm not there. And it's dark, and he's alone. No help, no one there, and he's lost, and he's helpless. And as long as that is a possibility—I couldn't stomach it. I couldn't handle knowing that he'd be alone."

Patty looked at her, a sad smile on her face. "If you feel you're in danger, I want you to call me. Right away, okay? I don't care what time it is, what the situation is. Okay?"

"Okay," said Bev. "It scares me. The Other—he seems to come out, more and more. Don wandered away, the other night, while I was in the shower. I thought he was asleep—I found him in the woods—"

"What was he doing out there?" asked Patty. "He didn't go to the cliff again, did he?"

"No, he—" Bev stopped. She thought about the hole, and the dog Gus, missing.

They'll come out, and they'll dig up that hole, Beverly. They'll find what's down there, and they'll take him away, and there will be nothing you can do about it.

"He was just wandering through the trees," said Bev. "And it was less than an hour. I don't—"

"I understand not wanting to put him in a home," said Patty. "But that doesn't mean we can't help you, okay? Whenever you need a break, you contact me, or Tim. Either of us can arrange for someone to come and give you a break, so you can relax for a spell. You're not a young woman anymore, Bev. Neither of us are. We have to know our limits.

Okay?"

"Okay."

"You ready to go back inside?" asked Patty. "I'm sure the waiter will be happy to see us."

"Yeah, I think so."

"We have the rest of the day," said Patty. "I'll do my best to keep your mind off things."

They went back inside, Patty slipping her arm through Bev's. They talked about everything that wasn't Don as they ate, and then they strolled through downtown and shopped for hours. Patty stayed true to her word. She had never been short on words, and she did her best to keep Bev's mind occupied with things besides Don, and The Other, and whatever was buried in that hole in the woods.

But Bev felt him creeping, in her mind.

The Other. He waited.

8

Don's trip with Tim was uneventful. Tim brought him back as the sun was setting, reporting nothing out of the ordinary, aside from Don having a few episodes of forgetfulness. A good day.

Bev was happy for him, happy for both of them.

But she was also jealous. Because The Other was back the next day. And the next. And the next.

He was unpredictable. He'd appear at any time of day, in any situation. Bev found herself on guard at all times, her mind always examining all of Don's actions, checking his eyes, seeing if the dark void of The Other stared out at her, or the pleasant familiarity of her husband.

The Other would never stick around for long. The darkness would come, linger for a moment, and then disappear, and Don would be himself again.

But the fear never left her.

His presence was always momentary, but she could never be sure where he was, or if the man who looked like her husband was actually Don or not. And she remembered the ominous laughter at the bloody news, and the anger in his eyes when she had turned it off. How he had enjoyed her fear.

And she didn't forget the shovel in the dark, and what was buried out in the woods, the knowledge she ignored in a box in her mind, anything to keep Don hers.

The Other appeared every day, and pushed his boundaries, finding new ways to inflict pain on her. She had sensed it with the laughter, a sense of performance in it, or targeted words, hurtful, where she was weakest.

Over days, she realized it wasn't accidental, or incidental. It was purposeful. Whatever this other personality was, it hated her. It enjoyed hurting her, laughing at not just pain, but at *her* pain.

She did her best to ignore The Other, to steer clear of him.

The question hung in the air, though. It remained in her mind, and The Other was happy with it unanswered.

The question was what if he challenged her? She had done her best to protect Don. To stop him from doing something negligent, or dangerous.

What if The Other stopped her?

For a few weeks, the question went unanswered. The Other came and went, leaving for hours and hours, and then appearing when she wasn't expecting it, delighting in pain and horror, and then disappearing again, leaving Don confused and her hurt.

He'd ask if The Other had been there, and she would nod, and he would struggle with guilt. So she stopped telling him. She would take all the pain. Bev couldn't imagine what was happening inside his mind, but it was already causing him enough turmoil. She would carry that burden as well.

The question went unanswered.

One night, she woke up to Don stirring next to her. His breathing went faster for a moment, and then he was awake, laying there. Bev knew Don's sleeping habits like everything else, with no mysteries left between them. But she didn't move or speak. She waited.

Don moved slowly, pushing his way out of bed, sliding out from under the covers, onto his feet. Still, she didn't move, keeping her breathing even, her eyes closed. He got up and left the bedroom, closing the door behind him.

Was it Don that had awakened?

Or was it The Other?

She lingered a moment longer, and then got out of bed, listening, her heart rattling in her chest. She heard him move softly through the house.

The back door. He was heading to the back door. Was he going to the woods?

She looked out the window, keeping the lights off, the light on their porch still on. The door opened with a small creak, and then Don left, walking down the stairs. If he was going back to the woods, she'd have to follow him. The image of him at the cliff hadn't been forgotten.

But he didn't head down the path to the forest.

Instead, he went to their big shed, on the corner of their yard, opening it, turning on the light, and then closing the door behind him. What was he doing in the shed?

She waited, minutes passing, and nothing changed. Minutes stretched to over an hour, and still nothing. How long could he stay in there? She wanted to go down there, to find him, but the fear and anxiety lurked in her gut, freezing her where she was.

What if he stays in there all night? Are you going to stay by the window for hours?

No, she wouldn't. She would go down there and confront him, whether it was Don, lost in his mind, or The Other, with whatever dark business he planned. She wouldn't let her fear control her.

She prepared herself to march down there, to face Don, but then the shed door opened, and Don came out, closing the door behind him, exactly as he found it, and then returned to the house. He glanced up to the window and Bev froze. She didn't think she was visible, but then his eyes were off the window and the back door opened, and Don came inside.

Get back to bed!

Bev moved quickly on the carpet, staying as quiet as she could, moving the few steps back to the bed, sliding under the covers, getting into a comfortable position, trying to calm her heart and have a consistent breathing pattern. She heard Don below her in the house, moving around, and then coming up the stairs.

She focused on her breath, and the bedroom door opened, and he came straight back to bed, slipping in seamlessly without noise or sound, the only evidence the subtle motion of their mattress. Within a few minutes, the familiar pattern of Don's sleeping was there, like nothing had happened, like his sudden departure was a dream.

He did the same the next night.

Bev watched him, just like before. Don got up, went downstairs, into the shed, and stayed inside for an hour before returning.

She returned to bed the same, waiting for him to return, to fall asleep again. Bev laid on her side, away from his part of the bed, so that he couldn't see her chest rise and fall with breath.

He slid into bed, and she waited for his breathing to return to normal before letting herself lapse into sleep, her eyes heavy. But he didn't. The dark voice of The Other instead spoke.

"Next time, stay in bed," he said, his voice heavy with intent. And then, within moments, Don's breathing was there again, Don asleep. Bev turned to look, and sure enough, his eyes were closed. If she woke him now, would he even know he'd been awake at all? Or was it The Other completely in control? Her heart shook her body, and she got out of bed and went into the bathroom, sitting on the closed toilet lid, her hands clasped over her face.

It took an hour for her breathing to slow. The threat was there. The Other didn't want to be bothered, didn't want to be watched, and had warned her. What would happen if she ignored it?

The Other didn't appear at all the next day. Was he resting? Or was Don fighting him off?

Stop it, stop it, Beverly. He isn't alive. There isn't another person inside Don. It's the disease making him do things. That's all it is.

But she couldn't stop planning against The Other. Even

when he was silent, and only Don was there, he stayed on her mind, even as Don spoke to her, or they watched television, or ate. She cursed herself, because The Other had stolen even more of their time together, with the dread and fear he inspired.

She thought to ask Don. If he remembered anything when The Other was active. If he had any control at all when this other personality surfaced. But she was afraid, afraid of hurting him, of exposing how helpless he was, how incapable he was of controlling anything.

So she said nothing and assured him everything was okay. She tried to keep The Other out of mind that day and enjoy her time with Don. They stuck to their normal routine. They did their crossword together, even if Don didn't know as many of the answers as he used to.

Despite her thoughts about The Other, he didn't show all day, which meant it was a good day. She kissed Don goodnight with hope in her heart that The Other was a simple blip on the radar, a darkness that would fade eventually in the light.

The Other woke in the middle of the night. He moved the same way as he had the past two nights, Don's consistent breathing changing into a calm wakefulness, leaving the bed, and then the room, without saying a word.

Bev laid there, hearing him move through the house, remembering the words of The Other from the night before.

Stay in bed.

Anxiety ached inside her, nausea almost overwhelming her. He would know if she got up, and watched him, but she couldn't afford to let him control Don, and do whatever he intended to do. If Don was in danger, she had to do something, even if it was to protect him from himself.

As she laid there, she expected to hear the familiar noise of the back door opening, and then of the shed. But instead, the front door opened, and then shut. And then the soft sound of a car engine turning on.

He was leaving.

Bev shot up out of bed, her fear forgotten, her heart pumping. Don couldn't leave, she didn't care how or what threat The Other had promised. She jumped out of bed as fast as her creaky body would allow, throwing on pants and shoes and grabbing her keys, running down the stairs as quick as she could. The car pulled out of the driveway and down the street as she looked out the front door.

She had to follow him.

Bev pushed through the front door, slamming it behind her, not caring about locks, running to her car and starting it up, reversing suddenly, barely missing the mailbox. She slammed the car into drive and floored it, her tires squeaking against the pavement.

As she turned down the street, she saw brake lights, and Don's car turn right.

Toward town.

She left her headlights off, using the streetlights to navigate. She hoped she didn't see anyone else on the road.

Bev followed, turning after Don, seeing his tail lights. The road went straight into town and was easy to follow. They were only a few miles from the city center, and Bev got closer to Don, close enough to verify that it was his vehicle. But she couldn't get too close, at least not until he had parked. It was too risky in the car. Who knows what would happen if Don regained control while The Other was driving. It was too dangerous. She kept her distance, just far enough back that she couldn't be seen. Or at least hoped she couldn't be seen.

Don continued straight for a few minutes more, and they entered the edge of town proper, where the stores, restaurants, and college were, where they had both worked for the majority of their life. Where they had met, and where they had lived until they got married.

He turned left, toward the growing Crestfield downtown area, filled with cute cafes, antique shops, and thrift stores the college students would raid every weekend.

Where is he going?

She turned, following him, just in time to see him turn down a side street, and she sped up, the streets empty this late, and then she turned to follow him, and she had lost him.

"Fuck!" she yelled, hitting the steering wheel. She drove forward, looking right and left at every intersection, hoping to see him.

Nothing, nothing, nothing, and then she looked left and she saw brake lights far down the street, and it was all she had and she turned, following. There was ample light here, and she would be seen if she got too close, regardless if she used her headlights or not. The brake lights were stationary, and she realized he had parked. She stopped, and pulled into a spot next to the curb. She killed the engine, waiting.

Finally, the brake lights turned off, and she saw a figure leave, three blocks up, hard to make out in the dim light of the night. They disappeared down an alley.

Bev got out, walking briskly, her knees still stiff. She pushed through the soreness, moving as quickly as she could, keeping her eyes up, looking for any movement. First, she would verify it was Don's car she had followed. Then she would follow him if it was. Within a couple minutes, she had made it close enough to confirm it was Don's car, the luxury sedan he had bought a decade ago. Where had he gone?

She went to what she thought was the alley he had ducked into. What was The Other's plan? Why was he downtown, in the middle of the night? There wasn't anything open, and there were no other people. It was four in the morning. The only place open was a coffee shop on campus, for students studying in the dead of night.

The alley was empty, leading to the next street over, and she hurried, but tried to stay silent, keeping her eyes peeled. Bev needed to find Don quickly, before The Other could hurt him, either intentionally or accidentally.

Bev came to the next street, and looked up and down, still seeing no one. Where did he go?

She stopped, listening for anything. She reached into her ear and turned up her hearing aid, to what would be uncomfortable levels. It would serve her now, and she listened. There was a rustling noise up the street, across it, from an alley, and she turned the hearing aid back down as she approached, peeking into it before heading in.

There was a light in it, flickering, a fire, and long shadows danced in the alley. Somebody was down there, and she crept toward them, hiding behind boxes as she went, her end of the alley dim. Bev stayed out of the light from the flickering flame. The noises got louder, and she soon saw the cause.

It wasn't Don.

A man shuffled around a ramshackle lean-to built from wooden pallets and other pieces of wood and plastic, a tarp tied over it. He was moving his meager belongings near the fire that was contained to a metal barrel, to keep him warm in the cool night.

Crestfield didn't have a large homeless population, but they did exist. Bev pitied them, and tried to help any way she could, but a majority of the city just wanted to ignore them.

But it wasn't Don. She would retreat, and try to pick up his trail.

But then she saw movement, not from the homeless man, but from beyond him, a shadow crossing through the flickering light of the fire. The homeless man didn't see it. Bev wasn't sure *she* saw it, but then it moved again, and now she knew something was there.

Creeping closer, and then his face came into the light.

It was Don.

No.

It was The Other. He came into full view of Bev, still behind the homeless man, a ghost in the darkness, moving quietly, his eyes hollow and dark. He carried something.

It glinted in the firelight, something metal and heavy, and then he raised it above his head, and Bev froze, her heart full of ice.

He brought it down on the homeless man's skull with a sickening thud.

And then again. And again.

9

Bev had just started her new assistant professorship at the school, and she hadn't expected Don home before her. But his beat up old station wagon sat in the driveway.

She found him inside their apartment, sitting at the coffee table with an open beer. Alarm bells rang in her mind. An open book sat in front of him. He stared at it, but didn't seem to be reading. Don didn't look back when she came inside.

"Don?" she asked. "Is everything alright?"

He didn't answer.

"Don?" she asked again, moving closer.

He moved now, glanced toward her, and halfheartedly smiled.

"I got a job offer," he said, before taking a swig of beer.

"That's great!" she said. She sat down next to him. "You're not acting like it's great, though. What's wrong?"

"I got a job offer," he said. "Assistant professor, at MIT."

"Holy shit," said Bev. "That's incredible! We should celebrate!"

He smiled and looked at her, his eyes still sad. He raised his beer. "That's what this is."

"What are you not telling me?" she asked.

"It's MIT, Bev," he said. "Boston. Two hours away, and that's without traffic. On a Monday morning, it would be three. I can't commute three hours, one way."

When he had said MIT, she had done the math, of course, in her head. But she wouldn't rain on his parade. And she wouldn't be the person who would hold someone back from what they wanted.

"I know neither of us has really talked about it," said Don. "We're both—we're both non-confrontational. I always figured we'd cross the bridge when we came to it. Well, here it is. There's a bridge in front of us."

She took her purse off, and placed it on the table, and reached out a hand to him, squeezing it. He squeezed back.

"I don't want to leave Crestfield," she said.

"I know you don't," said Don. "You haven't hidden it."

"I just got my job," said Bev. "And I like it here. It's the right size place for me. I don't get lost here. I can envision a life here. Boston—it's too big. Too much, too many people, too loud."

"I like Crestfield, I do," said Don, taking a breath. "But the opportunities for me here will always be limited. The school's focus isn't math, and it never will be. It's an afterthought. MIT is built for math, for my research. It's the job

I've always wanted."

"I know," said Bev, her heart sinking. She had envisioned this moment, in the dark, when a job would pull Don away, and she had steeled herself for it. But it didn't matter. It still hurt, hurt like hell, and it would get worse before it got better. "Don't let me hold you back. I want a life here. I want to raise a child here."

Don stared at her, his eyes as sad as she had ever seen them. Normally buoyed by happiness, now completely empty of it.

"I know," he said. He sighed and then took a swig of beer. "I'm afraid."

"Why are you afraid?"

He glanced at her eyes, and then looked back down at his hand that held hers. "Ever since I could remember, I knew what I wanted when I grew up. I know that for a lot of people, that's really hard. What they envision as their career changes, and changes again, and there's a constant war inside them for how they're going to direct their life. I've never had that. Since I was eight, I loved math, and math problems, and always wanted to chase that. I was lucky, and my parents and my teachers all pointed me in the right direction, and I made the choices that they laid in front of me. And I've kind of followed that without thought, because that's always what I wanted."

"Don, it's alright—"

"No, it's okay, Bev," he said. "Because living with you, being with you—it's made me think. And made me wonder about what I want. It made me *think* about what I want. About what that means. Because when you want something, it's self evident, right? You don't have to think about it—there's just an urge there, instinctual. If you really want something, your heart just pushed you there, without reason. And sure, you might compromise to get there, because you're human, and life is complicated. Even so, inside, there's no debate. You know it, like you know how to breathe. You want what you want."

"I don't understand."

"I don't want the job at MIT," said Don. "When I think about what I want to do with my life, my heart doesn't say take the job. It says to stay with you. I want you."

Bev felt a tear roll down her face, her heart bursting.

"What will you do here?" she asked.

"I'll find something to do at the school," said Don. "I'm sure I can. If not, I'll improvise."

"Don, please don't—"

"Bev, you're not holding me back. This isn't a compromise. I'm making the choice I want to make. Despite that, it feels like a half-measure. If you're going to do something, you go all the way."

Don finished off his beer, and stood up, and then kneeled next to Bev on one knee.

"Will you marry me, Bev?" he asked. "Sorry, I don't have a ring, not yet—"

Bev jumped off the chair and embraced him, both of them falling to the floor, tears streaming down her face. She kissed him, over and over.

"Yes, of course," she said.

10

Don brought the metal club down on the man's head, and Bev had a front row view, hidden in shadow, but able to see everything. She wanted to close her eyes, but she couldn't. Shock had taken her over and compelled her to watch the brutal murder.

Don rained down sickening, thudding blows onto the head of the man, the awful sounds of his flesh deforming, his skull cracking, of blood splattering up on Don's grinning face.

Bev saw it all, and she saw the glee with which Don inflicted this horrible, horrible violence. His mouth was spread wide, upturned into a huge smile, all his teeth show-ing. He breathed hard as he swung the club, well after the man was dead, merely driving the club into flesh. The club was a metal pipe, with weights crudely fastened to the end, and she recognized it from the shed. It's what he had spent his time on. This wasn't an accident, or done on impulse. This was planned, laid out, and formulated.

The Other knew he had wanted to kill, and had done exactly that.

Blood covered Don's face, and he finally stopped swinging, the homeless man long dead. Bev froze behind her cover, holding her breath in the silent alley, only the harried breathing of Don filling the space. The breathing soon stopped, replaced by a sound Bev recognized.

Don laughed, the same horrible laughter she'd heard the other day, that had filled their house not a week ago. It filled the alley now, The Other staring out of Don's eyes at the corpse of the man he'd just murdered.

The nausea hit Bev then, and her stomach roiled, their spaghetti dinner coming back up into her throat. She couldn't throw up, he'd find her, and God knows what The Other would do to her if he saw her here. Bev swallowed it down soundlessly, squirming with disgust, and forced down a shallow breath. She worried Don would see her, but he stared only at the corpse, before bending down, grabbing the body, and crudely throwing it over his shoulder, still holding the club in one hand. As he shifted the body, the victim's head came into view and Bev saw the damage done for the first time directly.

Bev's breath caught in her throat, and she forced the sound down, swallowing it as best she could, covering her mouth with her hand. Don paused, The Other searching the alley briefly with darting eyes, before giving up and turning, carrying the body away from the man's small encampment.

Bev watched him disappear into the shadows.

She waited until he was out of sight before she took a deep breath and cried, tears flowing down her face freely, unable to be stopped or dammed. Her hands shook uncontrollably as she wiped them away, watching her husband murder a random man in cold blood, her breath was coming too fast now, and she was hyperventilating, she knew she was, but no matter how much she tried to slow down her breathing it still sped up, and she took a shaking hand and slapped herself as hard as she could.

Bev blinked and forced herself to hold a breath. The slap hadn't been strong. She didn't have the strength anymore, but it had shocked her enough to breathe. She wiped away the tears, unsure of what she saw, or what to do.

You don't have time to think right now. You need to go home.

Alarm raised in her heart. She didn't know what Don would do with that body, but she had to get home before he did. If he got home before her, he would know she saw, and she'd be next. All the affection and love Don had didn't matter at all to The Other, and mattered less every day, as Don had less and less control. She looked one last time down the alley, and saw nothing, and got up, pushing her body past pins and needles and aching joints, and ran as fast as she could. It hurt, everything hurt, but she ran. It was only a few blocks to her car, and then she could go home, and get back in bed, and think about what to do next.

As she moved, the only thing she saw was the look on Don's face as he killed the homeless man, the absolute glee, the revelry in that terrible act.

Don would never have done something so horrible, so

evil. He couldn't. He was literally incapable of it. She had to squish all the bugs in the house, because he wasn't able to kill them himself. He couldn't even watch horror movies, because he was so squeamish. She remembered following him out of the theater during a showing of Braveheart, just because of the blood. They had stopped watching the news because the simple mention of violence would turn his stomach.

And now he had murdered someone, and Bev's mind tried to spin it away.

It was The Other. It wasn't Don.

But they were the same person, and Bev had done her best to ignore that fact, to treat this other personality as an invading force, but she couldn't anymore.

Bev reached her car, and she pushed all those thoughts out of her head. Get home, and then worry about the rest tomorrow. Just get home.

She started the car, turning on the headlights this time, and quickly pulled away, driving home as fast as she could. Her eyes darted from left to right, back and forth, looking for Don, searching for a shadowy figure carrying a corpse down the street.

But she saw nothing, the streets deserted so early in the morning. Her eyes went to her rearview mirror, seeing if Don would be behind her, in his car, still covered in blood, following her home.

But there was nothing, no cars behind her at all, and soon she was home. She pulled in, leaving her car in the exactly the same position as it was when she left. She closed the car door, locked it behind her, and ran inside.

Was the door locked when Don left?

She didn't think so, but she left it unlocked, less likely to be found out that way. She ran upstairs, and tossed all her clothes in the hamper, wearing her long nightgown, just like when she had gone to bed. If he looked in the hamper, he would know, but she didn't have time to do laundry. She laid in bed, trying to cool herself down, feeling the sweat rubbing off on the sheets.

Bev laid there, her heart pounding, doing everything in her power to calm herself down. She couldn't think about what she'd just seen.

About her husband killing in the night.

Of his personality disappearing.

Of her life falling apart.

She had to lie there, and force her breathing to slow.

She closed her eyes, and she listened. She waited.

Within fifteen minutes, she heard Don's car pull up in the driveway, his car door slam shut, and the front door open. She heard no hesitation.

He came up, his feet softly stepping on their well tread stairs. The bedroom door opened, Bev's back to it. She didn't turn to see Don, his face still covered in blood, or if it was his eyes, or The Other's that stared out at her. She stayed still, her breath even. The door closed, and he walked to the bathroom, going inside, closing the door behind him. The shower started, and she heard him wash up.

Bev pictured the blood falling off his face, soap and water wiping away any sign of the awful crime he'd just committed. All of it being washed down the drain. Was it Don in there, taking a shower, or still The Other? It had to be The Other, the person who had carefully planned out how to commit a random murder, simply for the pleasure of it, to vanish during the night, and come back to wash away the only evidence that tied him to the crime.

She laid in bed, not moving, keeping her breath as steady as she could, even as terror gripped her, a murderer a room over, a killer that was going to climb in bed with her. She felt herself shake, and no matter how she tried, she couldn't stop herself from trembling. Bev squeezed her hands into fists, doing her best to breathe steady, to put the terrible thoughts of the night away, to store them until tomorrow, when she could do something about it. When she would have the day-light to feel comfort in, when she could decide what to do about what her husband had become.

The shower stopped, and a few minutes later Don came out of the bathroom into the dark bedroom, the morning sun only slightly over the horizon. He slid into bed, just like he had the nights before. Bev braced herself for The Other's voice piercing the silence.

But there was nothing, and then the quiet sound of Don's breath as he eased back to sleep.

Bev laid there silent and still, her eyes closed. All she saw within was the smile on Don's face as he clubbed a man to death.

11

She didn't fall asleep, hearing Don sleep next to her, dreading that The Other would wake up and crawl out of bed again.

But he didn't. Don slept, his breathing even. Bev laid there until the sun painted the Earth with light, and then got up and started her normal morning routine. She'd have a few hours to herself. She knew it didn't make any sense, but it felt like the sunlight protected her. Daylight cast a ward against The Other, that would limit his influence and give her protection.

She made her morning coffee, and as she drank it, she thought. The shock of the night before had largely worn off, and she was as clearheaded as she could get.

What could she do?

That man was dead. She had watched him die in front of her, killed by Don.

It wasn't Don. It was The Other.

She knew it wasn't Don's personality that did it. Some side effect of the disease had caused it to alter, to shift, for a part of his brain to die, and another part to compensate, and that part was awful, was evil.

But it wasn't Don. It wasn't the man she knew, and she couldn't treat Don like The Other, and vice versa. She wouldn't allow The Other's behavior, no matter what it was, to make her hate Don, the man she still loved.

That doesn't make a difference, and you know it.

He had murdered a man, whoever was behind the steering wheel. He had killed Gloria's dog, Gus, buried out in the woods, and she had tried to ignore it, to avert her eyes and hope hard enough that it wasn't true, and now a man was dead, and it was her fault—

You didn't kill him, Bev.

She could have stepped in, reported Don's involvement with the dog, and that man would still be alive.

You don't know that. You couldn't have known that. You've loved Don for forty years, you can't just twist on a dime and change everything—

She pushed it all out. What should she do now? She couldn't stay like this, they couldn't stay like this. A man had died, and she feared for her life in her own home.

You know what will happen if you turn him in.

Bev saw it clearly, in her mind's eye. The authorities would take him away, and there'd be court cases, and Don would be tried for murder. They would hire lawyers, who would have to fight for the fact that Don wasn't culpable for his actions, and his reward, if they succeeded, would be spending what remained of his life in a guarded mental health facility, away from her, away from freedom, and away from anything he once remembered. He would live the rest of his life in a fog, not seeing anyone he loved or cherished, except for her sparse visits.

If they won. If they failed, he would go to prison, who treated men like animals, and Don would get locked up in a cell, with his disease completely untreated. It would be hell.

The image of the man dying flashed through her mind, over and over. And she knew that it was a precious life, and the horror of the moment would live inside her for the rest of hers. But he wasn't her husband. He wasn't the man who she had loved for over forty years, whom she had sacrificed for, who she had built her life around. Who she had suffered with, and for, for years and years.

She was in a nightmare.

Bev knew she should go to the police. She should tell them what happened and let the authorities figure it out.

But once she gave them control over Don, she would never have it again. And what if The Other never showed again? She pictured Don, confused, in a jail cell, in prison, for the rest of his life. The doctor had said Don might only live another year.

What if he was wrong? What if Don lived ten more years? A decade of his life, his mind deteriorating, facing the misery of a jail cell?

She didn't know if there was a crime that Don could commit that would compel her to give him that life. He had lived over seventy years as the best man she'd ever met. The disease had killed that man. The Other had killed that man.

Bev took a long swallow of coffee and rubbed her tired and weary eyes. Her mind was full of hornets, the traumatic night, the lack of sleep, the stress, the horror, all of it weighing on her. It made thinking hard, everything difficult. Her stomach ached at the thought of any choices she would have to make.

If she asked Patty, or any of their close friends, they'd all say the same thing. Talk to the police. Talk to the authorities. Come out with it, and we'll do what we can.

And no matter how Bev hated the idea of it, she knew it was the right thing. But she couldn't do that, not yet. She needed the opinion of the person she trusted most in the entire world.

Bev needed Don's opinion.

She knew he didn't remember what he did, or even realize that he was gone at night, The Other taking his body for joyrides, to eke out sadistic pleasure on dogs and homeless men. But he deserved to know, while his mind still functioned. He should have a say in his own destiny.

Bev waited. Don woke up, starting his own morning routine, and they went about their day, as normal as usual. Bev kept a close eye on him, waiting for him to be awake, and making sure The Other was firmly under lock and key. She would break the news to him while it was Don. The man who would understand. The man with compassion and empathy, who loved her. He would help her decide. Even if she already knew what he would say.

It was the middle of the day, after lunch. They had eaten sandwiches on the patio, enjoying the cool weather. A rabbit had scampered through the yard. Bev tried her best to shove the horror from the night before deep in a corner of her mind, to enjoy the moment with Don. Because they would be few and far between after this.

They went inside and sat on the couch. Don went to turn on the TV, but Bev stopped him.

"We need to talk, Don," she said.

He looked at her with concern.

"What's wrong?" he asked. "Did I—"

She raised a hand to him, and then reached to his own, squeezing it softly, warmly, holding it.

"I need you to just listen," she said. "Okay?"

"Okay."

"Do you remember anything strange about the past few nights?"

He looked at her, his eyes shining. "No. I remember going to sleep, our normal routine. Why?"

"That's what I thought," she said. She took a deep breath. "You've been going out at night."

"What? What—"

"Just listen," she said. "You've been waking up early, early in the morning, and slipping out of bed. At first, you were going into the shed, and spending an hour or two there, before returning."

She squeezed Don's hand and felt a tear trickle down her face. She wiped it away. "I watched you. I didn't know what to do. I haven't said anything—but The Other. He's been more active. More and more, he shows himself. But I think those all were distractions. Because the next night, he warned me. He warned me to stay in bed. To not watch, to not follow."

"I don't—"

"I know, you don't remember," said Bev. "It was the shed

again. And then a third time, he got up, and out of bed, in the middle of night. Or the early morning. This morning. And this time, he—you—went for a drive."

"No—"

"Please," said Bev. "And no matter what he said. I couldn't let you drive off without following. I wouldn't let you hurt yourself. I couldn't let you go without trying. So I followed. I followed you downtown, Don. You parked downtown, and got out, and I followed you—"

Her breath caught in her throat, and Don looked at her with concern and care, his soft empathetic eyes reading her.

"You killed a man, Don," she said, finally, forcing the words out. "I watched you beat a man to death. A homeless man. You killed him, and you carried his body away, and then I rushed home, so The Other wouldn't know I saw. But I saw."

"What?" asked Don, his eyes wide. "What—I killed—I can't—"

He let go of her hand, staring at her, and then stood up, pacing back and forth.

"Please, Don, calm down—"

"Calm down?" he asked. "You're telling me I killed someone, and I don't even remember it!"

"Please, I need your help—"

"Why didn't you stop me?"

"Stop you?" she asked. "How would I stop you? You have no idea what you're like when The Other is in control. He built some sort of club out of materials in the shed, and beat this man. He would have—"

"Attacked you?" asked Don. "No, that's impossible. I would never do such a thing. You've stopped me before—

I'm—I'm going to be sick—"

"Please, just sit down," said Bev. "I didn't want to go to the police until I talked to you about it—"

"Are you sure you saw me do it?" he asked. "It's not possible it was some nightmare—"

"Do you think I imagined all of this?" she asked. "You told me yourself that he scared you."

"I don't remember it, Bev!" He wiped tears from his eyes. "I don't remember any of this! I don't know what to do. I'm trying to be myself, but I can't even find him. When I dig deep inside, there's nothing there—and now—and now I'm a murderer?" He sighed, and sat down again, his head in his hands.

She sat down next to him and put her arm around him.

"You needed to know," said Bev. "I couldn't keep you in the dark. You deserved to have some say about what we do."

"What do you mean, what we do?" he asked, his voice quiet.

"I mean, I wanted to talk to you before we go to the authorities," said Bev, speaking softly.

"The authorities?" he asked. "For a murder I don't remember committing?"

"We have to do what is right," she said. "Even—even if it will be hard."

"That is easy for you to say," he said, his voice growing louder. "You will not be the one in prison!"

"Don, please," she said. He still hadn't looked at her again.

"No!" he said. "I do not believe you. I did not kill anyone."

"Don, I saw it," said Bev. "I know it's hard—"

"I do not care what you think you saw, I do not believe it!" yelled Don, his voice a growl. "I am not going to turn myself in for a crime I do not even remember happening!"

"Don, please—" she said, trying not to cry, but feeling the tears well up in her eyes. "I'm trying—"

"Trying what?" asked Don. "Trying to make this even more hard on me? You have no idea what it is like, Beverly!"

Wait a minute.

She looked up then, into his eyes, and she shifted away, pulling her arm back from him like she would a rabid dog.

"You haven't called me Beverly in forty years, Don," she said.

Then a familiar, awful sound erupted from Don's chest. A horrible, terrible laughter, deep, barking, and joyful in its depravity.

The Other.

He stared at her, smiling, a shark's grin. His voice erupted from Don. Dark, and low, and containing malice.

"I guess it is time we talked."

12

Bev jumped back, away from him, her eyes searching anything to defend herself with. She grabbed a lamp, and held it out, as if to ward off The Other.

There was no doubt it was him now, maybe had been him for the entire conversation, waiting for her to try to tell Don the truth and then playing with her. She stared into his dark eyes with fear.

He only smiled, a smile that Don had never worn in his entire life. He stared at her, but didn't move, staying on the couch, coiled like a snake. His hollow eyes considered her, even as she held the lamp in front of her.

"Please, Beverly," he said, his voice low, and sinister, lower than she thought Don's voice possible. Everything about him was unrecognizable. She barely saw Don at all, a monster now piloting her husband. "Please, I only wish to speak. If I wanted to harm you, that lamp would not be sufficient."

Bev stared at him, putting the light down.

"Don!" she yelled. "Don, come back! I want to talk to Don!"

The Other chuckled. "Don is unavailable at the moment. And no matter how much you beg or plead, there is only me. Like I said, I want to talk. I can hold on for a long, long time, if I make that choice. I would sit down, if I were you, and take your medicine."

Bev stared at him, a rage building in her, an anger she'd never felt toward Don in her entire life. The Other gestured at the recliner. "Please. We need to make some things clear."

"I won't speak to you," said Bev.

"Fine," said The Other, his voice a low growl. "Tonight, I jump off the cliff in the forest. I will ensure Don dies an awful death. He will come to the surface right after I have leaped."

His dark eyes were full of brutal honesty. He would do it. "Sit," he said.

Bev stared, and then took the seat across from him, her body tense, ready for anything.

"I will not attack you, Beverly. Not now. You do not need to be on edge."

Bev bristled. "How dare you. I watched you murder a man last night."

"I know," said The Other. "Do you think me a fool? I know everything that Don knows, and he knew that you would never, ever let me wander alone." He smiled, and then laughed.

"How could you?" asked Bev.

"It felt incredible, Beverly. The blood on my face." He breathed a deep breath of pleasure. "There is nothing like it, in all my years, that can compare. The feeling of flesh giving way, of the sound of a death rattle, of human life escaping a body. The *sense* of a soul slipping away."

All his years?

Beverly looked at him, his dark eyes full of glee, of joy, of just the memory of killing the homeless man.

"What are you?" she asked. "Why? Why has Don transformed into you? I don't—"

"You do not see how it is possible," said The Other, still smiling. "Have your thoughts focused on that idea, Beverly? That somewhere, deep down inside, Don was always capable of such terror? That he secretly lusted after murder and death and blood? That I am the worst of him, floated to the surface, all the safeguards he erected in his mind destroyed by some disease, eating away at his defenses against himself?"

The Other stared at her, waiting for her to answer. She said nothing, only staring back, unsure of everything.

Then he burst into that same dark laughter, braying until his lungs were empty, taking a great breath, and howling until he was out of air, staring at her the entire time. He was laughing at her.

"Do not be ridiculous," said The Other, his face serious, the smile and laughter gone just as fast.

"What have you done with my husband?" asked Bev. "I want him back."

"He calls me The Other," he said. "That is not who I am, but it is a title I do enjoy. You may use it, if you wish. I have been named many things, most forgotten by all human minds. The Usurper was most common, for a long time." He paused, and smiled. "I do enjoy The Other, quite a bit. It will serve."

Bev only stared. The doctor had said that other personalities can emerge from Alzheimer's patients. She had taken him at his word. That's all The Other was, no matter how scary he seemed. The disease had wrecked Don's mind, and this was a side effect. Scary, but not supernatural.

But as she looked into The Other's eyes, Don's eyes taken over, and heard him speak, all of that was thrown into doubt. Whatever this was, it wasn't Don, not even a small part of his mind. It was something else.

"Answer me," said Bev. "What are you?"

"It is so easy," said The Other, his low, hollow voice filling their house. "When their mind begins to go. It really ratchets down the difficulty. You can just *slide* right in. There is a hole to be filled, a vacuum that almost *pulls* me in. It is irresistible. It demands my attention. Your husband was an empty space, waiting to be filled. And I slipped right in."

"That didn't answer my question," said Bev.

"No," said The Other, smiling again. "There are no easy answers, Beverly. But you are smart. Don knows you are. You taught literature, did you not?"

Bev didn't answer. The Other's eyes looked up, accessing some information, and then looked at her again. "Yes, the classics. You have read Dante. Milton, Paradise Lost. You know of my kind. Not completely accurate, but close enough to get the picture."

Bev thought for a moment. Dante? Milton?

Her mind made the connection.

A demon? That's impossible.

"You do not believe me?" he asked. "Well, the alternative is that your husband is a murderer. Believe what you wish."

"What do you want from me?"

"I want you to keep your mouth shut," said The Other, his voice ringing.

"Excuse me?"

"You will not tell the authorities about the killing," said The Other.

"You killed a man in cold blood," said Bev. "I saw you do it. Do you expect me to stay quiet?"

"I expect you to value your husband's life," said The Other. "My threat is not empty. I can swan dive off that cliff, and leave your husband right before impact. He will suffer, and then he will die."

"You—"

"I have a convenient vehicle," said The Other. "But I can leave whenever I wish. I would survive, and Don would die, scared, and alone. I know you do not want that."

Bev took a deep breath, and held it, her anger rising. She wanted to throttle this thing, whatever it was, but it would only hurt Don.

"Or, you could tell the police, and point them in the right direction. They might eventually believe that a seventy-year-old man with no prior record was capable of murder. But by that point, it would be Don and Don alone facing the consequences. I would be long gone, again, leaving Don diseased, insane, and suffering."

"You son of a bitch—"

"Oh, no, please," said The Other, putting his hands out, palms forward. "You should restrain your anger. Any outbursts and it will be Don you will be yelling at. Not me."

"What should I do, then? Remain quiet, while you inflict more suffering?"

"Yes," said The Other. "Exactly."

"What do I get out of this?"

"You get what I give you," said The Other. "The more co-operative you are, the more time with your husband you get."

Bev felt tears roll down her face. "You're a monster."

"No," said The Other. "That is something else entirely. I like Don's mind. Analytical. Smart. He was a kind man, in life. I find causing pain in his body exhilarating. I do not wish to leave. Do not make me cause him harm."

"He doesn't deserve this!" yelled Bev.

The Other sighed, and then he was gone. Don's eyes were again his own.

"Bev?" he asked. "What's going on? Are you okay?"

She stared at him, unsure, her face wet. He stared back, confused.

"Bev?"

She went to him and embraced him, hugging him as hard as she could, crying into his shoulder. He squeezed her back, holding her tight.

"I'm sorry, Bev," he said. "I'm sorry this is what I've become."

"It's not your fault," said Bev. "It's not your fault." She squeezed him, holding his warmth close to her. Then The Other's voice whispered in her ear.

"Do not tell anyone," it said, and she let go, falling back onto the floor. Her heart was cold, she had hugged that thing—

Don's face looked back at her, unsure of what was happening.

"Bev?" he asked. "What's wrong?"

She stared at him from the floor. She said nothing.

13

"What symptoms are you suffering from, Don?"

"Memory loss, disorientation, confusion," said Don. "I lose track of time, or of what I was doing. Hit and miss. Some days worse than others."

"What day is it?"

"It's Tuesday," said Don.

"Time?"

"Uh—I think noonish," said Don. "I remember the appointment was for noon."

"Good," said the doctor. "I'm going to read a short list of words. I want you to listen, and then repeat them to me."

"Okay."

"Red. Dog. Van. House. Desk. Rhino. Aluminum. Xylophone."

Don looked at him. "Red, dog, van, desk—rh—rhino." He paused. He stopped and shook his head. "I think that's all I got, doc."

"Good," he answered. "I'm going to ask you to do some simple calculations. Answer as quickly as you can."

"Okay."

"2+2."

"4."

"3-2."

"1."

"9-2."

"7."

"10/2."

"Uh—5."

"12-9."

"Uh—um—"

"Okay, that's enough," said the doctor. The three of them sat in the small examining room, Don sitting on the butcher paper on the examination table, fully dressed.

"Alright, Don," said Baumann. "The nurse is going to take you and get some samples. Okay?"

"Alright, doc," said Don. A nurse came in as if on cue, opening the door and gesturing for Don to follow her. Don left wordlessly. Bev watched until he was out of sight. She had done the same since they'd left the house, as they got to the doctor's office, as the nurse guided them to the exam-ination room.

She had done the same since they'd woke up.

Since The Other had revealed himself, and declared both Don, and by extension, her, his hostage.

She had no seen no evidence of him since their talk.

Don's eyes had remained himself. His soft and delicate voice stayed soft and delicate, and he was only kind and gentle, like he had been their entire lives.

Bev had dreaded sleeping that night, even though she was exhausted, running on little sleep and lots of coffee, guzzling so many cups throughout the day that she'd lost count. She *had* fallen asleep, her body giving up the ghost, but she slept restlessly, her mind waking her up throughout the night, continually expecting Don to be awake, *no*, for The Other to be awake. For him to go out into the world, in the dark, and commit evil in her husband's guise, leaving Don with no memory.

But Don had slept through the whole night. She was the only one worse for wear.

Don had asked again that evening, if she would tell him what had happened. Why she had suddenly seemed so cold toward him? She had told him it wasn't a big deal. That she'd talk about it when she was ready. And he had taken that as an answer, even if it wasn't one.

And she had hugged him, and kissed him, after her eyes could tell that it was him. And she had tried to make it genuine, not for her, but for him, for Don, the man held captive by—by whatever The Other was.

Bev wasn't a good actor or a good liar. She never could hide what she really felt. And she was sure Don saw the difference. The Other won, no matter what she did.

She had heard him speak, she had, and he told no lies. None of it made any sense. But a monster? A demon? She was an agnostic, had been most of her life, but when you start talking about Hell, and demons, and angels, that's when you started to lose her. It was too much like the fiction she'd taught all her life. Characters, not real people. Forces of nature given personification, to make people feel better.

But what was The Other, then? Dr. Baumann had told her Don's personality might shift. And that, that she could buy. The Don she knew, changing.

But not like this.

So here they were.

Don left the room, and Bev's eyes stopped following him. The door shut with a ka-chunk. The doctor looked at her, and Bev stared back. Her exhaustion weighed on her.

"You alright, Bev?"

"I'm tired," she said. "Scratch that. I'm exhausted."

"You need to sleep more," said Dr. Baumann.

"I can't," said Bev. "I have to keep an eye on Don. Without me, he might—"

Kill someone.

But she trailed off instead.

"You won't be of any use to either yourself or Don if you're chronically exhausted," said Dr. Baumann. "It's not healthy. For either of you."

"I know, I know," said Bev. "Is there anything different about him?"

"As far as I can tell, he's the same as he was the last time you both visited," said the doctor. "Maybe a little more cognitive decline, but again, it's hard to say, even if you went and got another PET or MRI. The science on this is still so young. You said his behavior has changed?"

Bev stared at him. What could she say?

Yes, occasionally a dark entity overtakes him and commits foul murder. It calls itself a demon, Doctor. Is that on your list of symptoms?

"Yes," she said. She took a deep breath. "I mentioned The Other before. He's sprung up again, multiple times."

"Don had mentioned him when he was on the cliff side, before, correct?" asked Dr. Baumann.

"Yes," said Bev. "But it's different now. It's hard to explain. It's like he's a different person. His eyes change. His voice changes—"

He acts like the Devil.

"—I don't recognize him anymore."

"How often does this happen?"

"Not often," said Bev. "Once or twice a day. Sometimes not at all. But when it happens, it's debilitating. He is not Don, not at all. He is completely someone else. And that person is mean, and awful. He—" *What could she tell him?* "—he laughed at news coverage of a bombing in the Middle East. He thought it was funny, the pain and death."

Dr. Baumann stared at her. "Has he threatened you?"

"Not overtly," said Bev. *Another lie.* "But I don't feel safe around this other. *The* Other. He scares me."

"Beverly, I know I brought it up before, and I know you weren't interested then, but I have to ask." He took a breath. "It might be time to get him full-time care. Taking care of him is clearly running you ragged, and if his personality is shifting, he's probably better off with people that can take care of him long-term, and won't endanger you."

Bev looked down, and found herself crying. The doctor brought her a box of tissues and put an arm around her.

"It's a tough situation," said Dr. Baumann. "There's no shame in asking for help."

"It's not that. It's—" She wanted to say it was the fact that she didn't know what The Other would do, if she tried to take his fun away. Would he have Don commit suicide? Would he kill more, in Don's name? Or would he flee, in search of an easier victim?

She doubted it. But she couldn't tell any of this to the doctor. Telling him Don was possessed by a demon would only ensure Don being taken from her.

"What is it?" asked Dr. Baumann.

Bev sighed and said what she could.

"Don is all I've known for most of my adult life," said Bev. "Married for forty years, together for longer. I've constructed my entire being around him. Shaped myself around him, and our relationship. How am I supposed to just give him up? I can't just cut him out of my life like that. How can I stop supporting the man who's given me his entire life? How can I say, 'no, this is too much'? How can I surrender, no matter what I face, when what I lose is Don?"

Dr. Baumann nodded and took a deep breath, and sighed.

"I know," he said. "It's something patients and their partners face routinely when they're dealing with late-stage dementia. Don's not quite there yet, and this will be hard to hear, but you need to hear it." He paused. "There is no cure, and Don will not get better. His mind is deteriorating, and no matter how hard you push yourself, no matter how much you love him, there will be a time when you are no longer enough to take care of him. When he will be unable to remember your name, or your face, or your wedding anniversary. And there is nothing you can do about it. In many cases, patients are largely docile. Sometimes, the confusion can result in injuries to themselves. In rare cases, it can result in injuries to others, including their partners. Beverly, I know you love your husband, and he loves you. The last thing he would want is for you to get hurt, either from an accident, or from overwork and too much stress. You need to take care of yourself. And if something bad happens, there is no putting that genie back in the bottle. It is usually better to act before it gets too bad, instead of after."

"I can't give up on him, doctor," said Bev. "I won't."

No matter what's inside him.

"I can't say that such a dramatic personality shift is common," said Dr. Baumann. "Typically, it's a gradual process. Does he remember these instances at all?"

"No."

"Then he's further along than tests have shown. Regardless if you decide on full-time care or not, Beverly, I want you to keep your safety in mind. If you feel unsafe, if you feel threatened, you need to put yourself first."

Bev looked into his eyes for a moment, and then nodded, and then lied. "I will, Doctor."

"Just remember, the option is there," said Dr. Baumann. "I would advise you to make that choice before the choice is made for you."

14

She took Don home and tried to live a life. Tried to pretend that there wasn't something inside Don holding them both hostage.

It had been over a day since The Other appeared, since he had threatened the both of them. Maybe the visit to the doctor had scared him into hiding. She would take the break when she could get it. And the doctor was right about her pushing herself. She couldn't keep it up. She didn't brew the afternoon pot of coffee. The amount of caffeine she'd been taking had been astronomical and she needed to dial back. She'd have to fight through the drowsiness.

Don stayed mostly himself the rest of the day after the doctor. They tried to stick to their normal routine, and it seemed to work. They made dinner together, and it felt like a normal life again. The anxiety that almost never left her fell away. She breathed normally for a few minutes.

They ate dinner, and Don cracked a pun that made her laugh, and he smiled, and it was *his* smile, good-natured and sweet and she fell in love with him all over again.

They sat down to watch Wheel of Fortune and Jeopardy, like they did every night. Don always liked Wheel more, and she had always loved Jeopardy more. She had a better mind for trivia, but Don was better at thinking on his feet with limited information. It worked out well for them over the years, with both of them getting their time in the sun when they would play better than the other during their respective shows, with both of them getting upsets over the years.

Don had struggled lately, but it was a testament to him he still wanted to watch. He still enjoyed the challenge, even if his memory couldn't keep up.

As Pat and Vanna introduced the contestants, Bev felt her eyelids flutter, as her head hit the couch cushion. She forced them open, but the lack of caffeine was having a bigger effect than she had expected, and she felt them close again. Don's voice brought her back to consciousness.

"Bev?" he asked. "Jeopardy's starting."

Her heart jumped as she jostled awake, all too often being startled by The Other waking her, not Don. But her eyes flew open and she looked over to see Don's loving eyes, not the dark hollows of The Other. He knew she liked Jeopardy. He wanted to make sure she saw it.

"Thanks, honey," she said, smiling, trying to hide the unbound fear that had flown to her face.

Jeopardy still hadn't replaced Alex Trebek, and she didn't

recognize the host. It said he was a football player, and she didn't know him. He was alright, but he was no Alex. But no one was.

The short few minutes of sleep had given her a jolt of vigor, and now, with Jeopardy on, she felt energized.

They announced the categories, and she was happy to see "Literature" as one of them. Don smiled at her as they announced. She always ran the table in any literature categories.

The contestants bounced around, hitting Potpourri, and then Geography, and then some category named Purple Things. She usually liked the funny categories, but she and Don both struck out on that one. Don had yet to get a question right, but he was engaged, and that was all it took for her to smile. It was a good day for them, despite the dour news from the doctor. The Other was nowhere to be seen.

The contestant on the TV called out, "Literature, $200".

The card flipped over, and the host read the question. "In this novel, after learning there are no grownups, Jack says, "We'll have to look after ourselves."

Bev opened her mouth to answer, and then Don's voice filled the room. "Lord of the Flies."

"Wow," said Bev. "Good job, honey."

He wasn't nearly as well read as she was, spending most of his time reading non-fiction, and following math research. He'd read fiction if she pointed him at it, but he rarely sought it out on his own. Lord of the Flies was well known, a high school read for most. Bev kept her eyes on the TV.

The same contestant got it right, and called again. "Literature, $400."

The host. "Edgar Allan Poe led a 19th-century Gothic revival with stories like this supernatural tale about Roderick and his doomed family."

Bev started "The—"

"The Fall of the House of Usher," said Don, confidently.

"You're getting all of them, tonight," said Bev, the contestant answering again the correct answer.

"I know a lot of things, Beverly," said Don, but the voice was dark and deep, and she looked over at Don and he was The Other now, his eyes shining darkly. Her hands gripped the couch.

"Literature, $600."

"This book with a lamb-free title marked the first appearance of Dr. Hannibal Lecter."

"Red Dragon," said The Other. He smiled his shark's grin at Bev. "Do you think a doctor can fix me, Beverly?" His voice boomed, heavy and low. "Do you think Dr. Baumann can root me out?"

"Literature, $800."

"In the satiric 1729 "A Modest Proposal," this author suggested dining on poor Irish children to control poverty."

"Jonathan Swift," said The Other, even before the host had finished with the question, not once breaking his stare with Bev. "He is in Hell, burning for his heathenism. Trebek is, as well. He could not outsmart cancer, and he cannot outsmart hellfire."

Bev's heart thudded hard in her chest. She was trapped in his eyes, in his stare. She looked only at him, this thing she knew was a demon now, no doubt in her mind.

"Literature, $1000."

"Gregor Samsa is the human transformed into a giant

pest in this 1915 novella."

"The Metamorphosis," he said, and he laughed, and laughed, bellowing the same terrible laughter. "Human knowledge is so trifling. You live long enough, you learn everything. Do you think you can outsmart me, Beverly? Do you think that if you subject Don to enough tests, enough experts, they will find me, and excise me? An MRI scan will not find me. I am invisible, impossible. Do you expect science to understand?"

"Please—"

"Oh, do not beg. It is not becoming," he said. "I am beyond doctors, Beverly. I am beyond help. The sooner you realize that, the sooner your life will be that much easier."

Her heart caught in her throat, but she forced out the words.

"I won't just give up," said Bev, narrowing her eyes, squeezing the couch cushion.

"Oh?" asked The Other. He smiled again, his mouth wide open, as if getting ready to swallow her. "Do you know why I like Don's mind so much? Why it is so delightful to inhabit?"

Bev only stared.

"Love," he said, cackling. "It is love, Beverly."

"I don't know what you're talking about," said Bev.

"Yes, you do," said The Other. "You feel it too. Don knows, and so do I. You feel the love between the two of you. I seldom encounter it. It has been a century since I have felt it. Mmmm."

"Stop," said Bev. "Stop it."

"The sensation," said The Other. "You do not understand. You could not understand. You have no concept of me, or what I am. The pain, the misery—they are delicious, fulfilling. They are everything. But—" He chuckled. "But when combined with such a deep love and dedication, oh my. That is when they truly enrich me. When that pain, that horror—when it destroys something so precious. So rare. When it eats away at something so valuable to you. I chip, chip away at your love, and replace it with agony."

Bev stood up then, and ran to the corner, and grabbed the golf club there. She had put it there, pulled it from the garage, from Don's old clubs, the biggest club in the bag, and put it in the corner, just in case. Just in case she needed to defend herself. The Other didn't move. He only watched her.

"What is that?" asked The Other. "A golf club. Are you going to attack me, Beverly? Please, swing away. I will not defend myself. It is the only way you will remove me from Don. You should tell your doctor friend that. 100% effectiveness. Hit me in the skull, crack me open, and let the blood flow." He laughed. "Do it. Kill your husband. That would make both of you killers with clubs. Maybe they will let you off with self defense. You did just tell Dr. Baumann you felt unsafe. They would let you go. One old lady. They would not condemn you to prison."

Bev grabbed the club in two hands and moved closer. Tears streamed down her face, The Other in front of her, provoking her. She knew he was.

"It is the only way you will remove me, Beverly. Kill Don. Get it over with. Oh my God, it will be incredible. A moment to be cherished for some time." The Other smiled. "But you will not get me. I will be long gone. And maybe, maybe, you will never see me again. Here, alone, you will be at peace. Maybe. Or maybe, I will find a home in another friend. In Patty. Or in your neighbor, whose dog yapped and yowled as I slaughtered it."

"You son of a bitch," said Bev.

"You have not said a word, I will give you that," he said. "Remember that, Beverly. Remember."

"I'll kill you," said Bev. She gripped the golf club hard and raised it above her head. "I'll kill you."

"Swing, Beverly, swing away," said The Other. "Watch your form. It can be tricky. Here, I will make it easy." He climbed down from the couch, throwing the coffee table out of the way easily, onto his knees, in front of her. "On a tee. Swing as hard as you can, and end this."

Bev held the club above her head, her shoulders aching, staring at the hollow eyes of this thing that possessed her husband, and then she dropped the club. She couldn't.

"That is what I thought," he said, standing up, in her face, his hot breath hitting her. "Weak. Cowardly. The true nature of love."

"Why? Why are you doing this?" she asked, her voice quiet, tears trickling down her cheeks.

"Why does the scorpion sting?" he asked. "Because it feels good to hurt you. Now run, run away."

Bev stood there and stared at him, and then ran upstairs.

15

"I'm losing ground, Bev."

Don's voice woke up Bev in the middle of the night, and fear gripped her at the sound of it, even though it was his voice, not the dark bellow of The Other. She expected Him at any moment now, never letting her guard down. Bev slept fitfully, her body at the edge of the bed, as far from the man she loved as she could lie. She thought about sleeping on the couch, but she couldn't risk being too far from him. He might scale down the side of house during the night. Don's fitness was as worse as it had ever been, but The Other didn't seem bound to the limits of Don's health or body, pushing past the constraints of his strength or endurance.

So she slept in fits and starts in their bed, her body shying away from the smallest amount of contact from the man who was sometimes her husband.

"Don?"

"I can feel it, inside. It pushes and pulls, and even when I can't remember, I can feel him there," he said, speaking out into the dark.

"Who?" she asked, even if she knew the answer.

"The Other," he said, his voice soft, like it always was, almost musical. "He's been taking over more, hasn't he?"

"Yes," said Bev. "I don't know how to tell you—"

"I know," said Don. "It's hard. I can't explain it. Some of it is the disease, I'm sure. And that's hard enough. But knowing—knowing that things will be hard, won't make me remember your favorite color. But The Other—"

"The Other is something different."

"I see it in your face," said Don. "You don't trust me anymore."

"I trust you—"

"Maybe you trust the me before this."

"I found you at the edge of a cliff—"

"I don't mean that," said Don. "You haven't kissed me in weeks, Bev."

A silence settled into the darkness of their bedroom. Bev finally spoke.

"I want to. But he comes out of nowhere, and as much as I love you—more than anything—I hate him. I hate him, more than I've hated anything. And if I kissed him—I don't know if I could stand it."

"I can't control him," said Don. "No matter what I do. It's like fighting the ocean, but that ocean is inside my head. The tides go in and out, and while they're out, I can walk on that dry land, and even dig a hole, and plant a tree. But as soon as I'm done, the tides come back in, and no matter how many walls I build, or dams I lay, the tide washes away that tree. Washes away my footprints. I can't fight him. He's liquid. He's invisible. I can feel—something inside of me, but I can't even see it."

Bev turned toward him, inching closer to his side of the bed. "I don't know how to tell you—"

"I know," said Don. "He's done—he's done bad stuff, hasn't he?"

Bev felt a tear come up, and she wiped it away in the dark. "Yes."

"I don't remember anything," said Don. "It's hard to tell what's real, Bev. Is this happening? Or is this a memory?"

"Oh, Don," she said, and she couldn't stop herself. She slid over to him and held him, squeezing him tight. She knew The Other might emerge, that this all might be a bait and switch, but she held him anyway, his warmth and touch feeling like a golden salve. A heavy weight relented inside her, and in that moment, she felt peace again. "This is real. *We* are real. And no matter what happens, I'll be here for you. I'm sorry, I'm sorry, I'm sorry."

He turned, and hugged her, and kissed her, and she kissed him back, and she felt human again, and she brought him close, and they embraced. The fear of The Other remained, but it shrunk, forced back into a corner of her mind. She would not let that thing rule her life. She wouldn't let it torment Don, not at all waking hours, not when it wasn't present. When The Other wasn't there, this *was* still her husband, this was still Don, the man she loved.

"No, I'm sorry," said Don. "I'm sorry that I'm doing this to you—that I can't control—" He shook, sobbed, and Bev held him as he cried. She felt tears come, and she cried with him, both holding each other.

"It's not your fault," said Bev. "I'm here for you. I always will be."

"I know," said Don. "That's what I wanted to tell you, Bev. What I needed to tell you, when I still could. I don't know—I don't know how much longer I'll be able to."

"Be able to what?"

"Be able to talk to you," said Don. "The tides. They come higher every day, and soon, there won't be a beach at all. And on that tide, The Other comes in, every time. He's there, underneath the water, surfacing when I can't fight back. And I can't see him, or struggle, or do anything. And—and I don't want to live like that."

"Don—"

"No, Bev," said Don. "If it comes to that, send me away. I think you knew anyway, but here it is, my permission. I don't want to be whatever it is. Because I can feel it, feel its energy. And it's terrible. It's like—like chaos inside. I can feel the hate, like an aura. I don't know, it's hard to explain, and I don't have the words—" He sighed. "But please—please, if he keeps taking me over. Do whatever is necessary to protect yourself. Do you understand?"

"Don—"

"Do you understand?" he asked, his voice as stern as it ever was.

"Yes," said Bev, as they held each other in the dark.

"Because it wants me, Bev. What am I supposed to do?"

"I don't know," said Bev.

"I don't either," said Don. "I didn't think retirement would be this. I thought—I thought we had more time."

16

They got back from the doctor's office. It was a few days after Bev's 41st birthday. They had both taken the day off from work for the appointment, and Don changed as soon as they got home into some gym shorts and a spare t-shirt, and went to work on the yard.

He had held her as she cried after the appointment, and had held her hand on the drive home, trying to change the subject to anything, anything that would keep her mind off what the doctor had told them.

But she was worried about him. Don kept to a pretty strict schedule for their lawn maintenance, almost always mowing and trimming and leaf-blowing on Sunday, every other Sunday, for the past ten years, settling into the rhythm after they'd bought the house.

But it was Wednesday, and he went to work in the yard, even in the late spring heat. He had remained stone-faced after the doctor had delivered the news. Don wasn't the most emotive man on the planet, but he wasn't afraid to cry, and would often cry more or more quickly than she would.

But not today. He had showed nothing, had hugged, had reassured her, and then had retreated into their backyard, the noise of the lawnmower engine spinning up not too long afterward.

Something was wrong, and she knew it. She couldn't bury herself in work when she was upset. Sadness devoured her, overtook her life, and it wouldn't let up until she conquered it.

So she sat on the couch and stared ahead, and all the anxiety and the worry and *all the thoughts* crossed through her, arcing in her mind, bouncing around like bees in a nest, thrumming, humming, and she did nothing, waiting for Don to come inside and find her there. She had to talk to him, but this utter sadness had stolen all her trust and courage in him, because this *was* the breaking point, the only thing that would rot them, erode them away from the inside out.

Bev finally got up, and she went outside. She needed to move, needed to do something. She walked through their backyard, past where Don was working, and down the path in the forest. Her feet moved, and she sweated as she walked quickly. She had a destination in mind, and as long as she walked, the thoughts couldn't keep up.

She finally saw the bench at the cliff side, and she let out a deep breath as she sat down. The sun pierced the canopy. It was beautiful.

"God almighty, it's roasty toasty outside," said Don, walking up behind her. She heard him, but didn't answer. She didn't know what to say. "Bev?"

Still she didn't answer, and then she looked up at him, covered in sweat, his shirt sticking to him, and she couldn't stop herself, and she started crying again, and before the tears could overwhelm her, she put her head back in her hands, as if to stem the tide.

Don said nothing, just sat next to her and embraced her, still covered in sweat. She didn't care, the touch was all she wanted, enough reassurance, enough for now.

"I'm sorry," she said, into his shoulder. "I'm sorry."

"Sorry for what?" he asked. "You don't have to be sorry for anything."

"I'm sorry for keeping you here," said Bev. "I'm sorry for holding you back. Holding you back for nothing."

"Oh, darling," he said, and brought her close again. Her insides burned, full of hollow ache and pain. "You haven't held me back."

"Yes, I have," said Bev. "You'd be at MIT, doing research. Probably a full professor there, with tenure, doing whatever you wanted to do. But I wanted to stay. I wanted a family. I wanted to stay in Crestfield. And you didn't. You stayed for me. Don't lie to me. I know it's true. You could have been something more."

"No," said Don, holding her closely. "I could have been something *else*."

"Something better," said Bev.

"Who decides that?" asked Don. "Who decides what's more valuable?"

"It's my fault," said Bev. "You heard the doctor. I can't

have kids. I won't have kids. Ever."

"We can keep trying—"

"I'm not holding out for a miracle," said Bev. "I believe the doctor."

"We could always adopt."

"Neither of us wants that," said Bev. "And it wouldn't be fair to the child."

"Even so," said Don. "It's not your fault. You didn't do anything wrong."

"I held you down," said Bev. "With the promise that we'd raise a family here. But instead, nothing. You stayed here for nothing."

He pushed her away, with two hands, and then held her at arm's length, his hands firm but gentle. He looked at her in the eyes. She met them for a moment, but couldn't hold his stare, and looked down.

"Bev, look at me," he said. She looked up again, into his eyes.

"I stayed here for you," said Don. "That is the beginning and the end. I stayed here, and married you, and when I married you, I married the you at every step along the way. When we got married, did you think everything would work out, along the way? That no matter what we wanted, everything would be fine?"

Bev looked at him. "No, of course not."

"No," said Don. "Neither did I. I married you with my eyes open. I knew it wouldn't be all smooth sailing. I knew there'd be bumps in the road. And I also knew that none of them would make me stop loving you."

"This is different. This is—"

"It hurts," said Don. "And it will hurt, for a long time. For both of us, in different ways. But that doesn't mean either of us have wasted anything. We've made memories together. We've traveled. We have friends, and family. We have each other. We have this house, we have everything we've built together. Right?"

"Yes," said Bev.

"*You* is all I ever wanted," said Don. "When I chose to stay in Crestfield with you, it's because I wanted you. And that hasn't changed. Children, a family—I wanted them too, but I wanted them with you. And nothing about that has changed either. You're still here."

"I feel like I'm letting us both down."

"If you could have a baby, you would," said Don. "But everything else is out of our control. *We* have done as much as we can. We're a team, right?"

"Yes," said Bev.

"I love you," said Don. "And I always will."

"I love you, too."

17

A crash woke Bev in the night, the sound of destruction, of something heavy falling. She scrambled up, her back complaining, telling her to slow down, but she forced herself up, and realized she was alone in bed. Too, too tired, and now she couldn't even wake when The Other got out of bed to cause mayhem and chaos.

It was The Other, assuredly. But why the destruction? Bev had a terrible thought, that maybe it was just Don who had gotten up in the middle of the night, and he wandered downstairs, and caused damage because he was confused.

"Don?" yelled Bev. There was no answer, but then, there was another loud crash, and then the sound of a door opening. Bev scrambled from the bed and grabbed the baseball bat in the corner before continuing downstairs. She had tucked it behind the corner curio, just in case, just in case The Other attacked her. She didn't think she could hit Don with it, even if The Other was in control, but—but she wanted the option if it came to it. If The Other got tired of toying with them, and just decided to bludgeon her to death, like he had the poor homeless man.

They had found the body, eventually, but there was no evidence there, at least none that made the news, and no suspects had been detained. No police had contacted them, and she doubted they would. The Other had covered his tracks well enough.

You could turn him in.

No, she couldn't. The guilt resided in her, piercing through her whenever she thought of the terrible sound the impromptu club had made when it hit that poor man, but it was guilt she could live with, whatever alchemy her conscience did that could bear the crime that had been committed.

If she had thought about it, she believed The Other, when he said he would make Don suffer. And as cold as it was, her love of Don provided for a lot of suffering to others before she would let him take the brunt of it.

Including herself.

She grabbed the bat and hurried downstairs to find the house torn apart. Bookshelves had been toppled over, the contents dumped all over the floor. The television was destroyed, and their big couch had been upended. She didn't know how Don had the strength to do such things.

The Other did it, Beverly. The Other wasn't bound to laws of physics.

She didn't have time for this. She didn't know why he had

destroyed the house, but she had to find him, to follow him, to try to limit what he would do this time—

Like you did last time? Like when you stared and watched and did nothing as he murdered a man?

A stab of guilt sliced through her, but she swallowed it down, tonight would be different, she wouldn't let him do it again, she would stop him.

She glanced out the front window, and saw both their cars in the driveway, and realized the door she'd heard was the back door. The threat wasn't to others. It was to Don himself. The silhouette of him against the sky, right on the cliff's edge, back on their anniversary, when this had all started—

That's not true, it had started before that—

She silenced her thoughts and moved as fast as she could to the back door, and then through it, onto the back patio, and the still night air was interrupted by harsh, barking laughter, and she recognized it as the laughter of The Other.

It echoed across the field behind the house, and then stopped, and then a terrible scream ripped through the air, and that wasn't The Other. That wasn't The Other at all. That was Don, a sound from him she'd never heard before, of utter terror, the sound of a man rising to the surface, confused, and lost, being taken from his home by some demon, piloting him out into the woods beyond his control.

Bev grabbed a flashlight and the bat and hurried off the patio, and into and out of the backyard. The screaming stopped, and then the laughter started again, that terrible, barking, bellowing noise, a sound Don was not capable of, his vocal cords, his lungs, stretched, the monster inside him pushing his body past human limits.

Because there was no doubt in her, all of it eroded away. Whatever that was inside Don, whatever The Other was, it wasn't natural. It had called itself a demon, and that was a good enough name for whatever it was, because it was laughing at Don's screaming, allowing his consciousness to surface long enough to scream bloody murder, and then sinking it back down so it could laugh, laugh, laugh.

The wind rushed past her and she couldn't hear the laughter anymore, the wind pushing it away, and then the thunder roared and the first raindrops fell on her, and God, the forest would be a muddy mess, and then the sky opened up, the rain pouring down.

She looked back, at the halo of light cast on their back patio. She could get an umbrella, or a poncho, or her rain boots.

The wind stopped for a moment, and she heard Don's scream again, and she didn't have time, and she rushed forward, the rain cutting through the beam of the flashlight. She ran behind it, as fast as her aching body could carry her.

Before she hit the forest, she was soaked to the bones, and then she was under the treetops, and the rainfall wasn't as bad, but it was darker, the trees capturing all the sound, and all the light. She followed the trail, moving as quick as she could, the ground softening underneath her feet.

The path had once been an old creek, and it always flooded when it rained, and even after a few minutes it was already slippery, and so she slowed down, because if she went any faster she would fall, and possibly hurt herself, and that would do no good for anyone.

She had stopped hearing the screaming, and the laughter, the rain too loud, the trees stopping too much sound from going anywhere. Still, she wouldn't let The Other do this without trying to stop him. It was doing it on purpose, punishing Don, pushing its limits. It had threatened her with ruining their lives, but what was the worth of it if it did it anyway?

The rain penetrated the treetops, big drops of water falling from the leaves above, and thunder boomed around her, the sky lighting up briefly and then darkening again. She was halfway down the path, and still saw no sign of The Other, of Don, but she knew where they would be, and she pushed through the punishing weather, a brief sound of a scream punching through all the noise.

It hurried her, even as the ground beneath her slid underneath her feet, and soon she was at the cliff, and the lightning flashed and she saw the same silhouette against the dark sky, Don, standing at the edge of the cliff.

"Don!" she yelled, as loud as she could, approaching him from behind, wary. "Don!"

She approached, only a foot away, the baseball bat still in her hand, ready for him to attack her, for The Other to turn, for its hollow eyes to stare through her, to charge at her, to try to throw her off the cliff. She could picture it, falling off the cliff, dying, Don being imprisoned, and The Other fleeing into some other victim, to raise hell and cause pain somewhere else.

But Don turned and she saw his eyes in the glow of the flashlight, both of them standing in the rain, the thunder crashing once more. It was him, only him.

"Hi, Bev," he said. He was soaking wet, still wearing his pajamas, a bruise forming on his face, Bev guessed from something in the destruction inside the house. He turned from her, and looked back out into the darkness beyond the cliff. No sunlight pierced through the canopy. The bench sat behind them, unoccupied.

"Don, let's go home," said Bev.

"Why?" he asked. "Maybe I should jump. Maybe we'd be better off. Maybe you'd be better off."

"No," said Bev. "You can fight this. We can fight this."

"It's a long road, Bev. And it only goes downhill. Down there, at the bottom of the cliff. That's what's waiting for me, even if it's not tonight. Even if it isn't The Other. Why prolong it? We can't stop it."

"Yes, we can," said Bev. "We can find a way. I'll find a way. Do you trust me?"

Don turned again, and looked her in the eyes, his gaze full of sorrow. He blinked once and nodded. "Yes," he said. "Of course."

"Then let me try and find a way out," she said. "I can do it. I will do it." She dropped the baseball bat, and then extended her hand out, reaching for him.

He looked down at her hand, and grabbed it, and then squeezed, Don's hand gentle.

"Let's go home," said Bev, and then Don's grip squeezed harder, squeezing tight, and soon the horrible laughter of The Other erupted from him, laughing into her face. The Other pulled her to the edge, next to him, even as she struggled, but his strength was too much, a vice on her hand.

"Yes, let us go home, Beverly," said The Other, his voice a bellow in the storm. "Let us listen to Don. Let us jump. We can end it, so quickly." It laughed, the terrible laughter, and she felt it vibrate through her, as it squeezed her. She tried to pull away, but there was no way, it was too strong, stronger than Don ever could be.

"Let us jump together," said The Other. "Two dead. Apparent double suicide. Or maybe Don pulled you. Or you pulled him. The world would never know. But it is a way out. You can go out together. Romeo and Juliet. True love."

"No, no!" yelled Bev, trying to pull away.

"There is no cure for me, Beverly," it bellowed. "There is no way to remove me. No surgeon, no doctor, nothing. I am forever. You want me gone? Jump, jump together, and I will be gone before you hit bottom. It is the only way. Jump, Beverly!"

She stared out into the darkness. No, no, she couldn't, she wouldn't. She wouldn't give up on Don. She pulled, and finally, The Other let go, and let her pull away from the cliff. She fell into the muddy soil of the path.

The Other stared at her, her flashlight pointed at its face.

"You can end this at any time, Beverly. You choose to prolong Don's suffering. You choose."

18

The Other had walked back to the house and gone back to sleep, leaving her out in the rain.

She had followed, picking up the baseball bat, but it was right. She would never hurt Don, not when she knew he was still in there, no matter what The Other did.

But she didn't forget the promise she made to Don. She would get it out of him.

And The Other was right on one other thing. A doctor wouldn't be able to remove him. He disappeared under the eyes of medical science, of a PET or MRI. He was merely a symptom of Alzheimer's to the doctors, who hid, turning invisible when anyone but Bev looked. If there was a medicine that would eradicate it, she doubted they could ferret it out in time, or not kill Don in the process.

But she wouldn't give up, not on Don.

She had called Tim, to take Don on another fishing trip. Tim had been happy to, and Don had hugged and kissed her before they went. He was more himself, but the shadow of The Other hung over everything for both of them. The Other hadn't presented itself to anyone but her, and she doubted it would with Tim. The trip was almost a guarantee of peace for Don and for her.

She watched Tim take Don in his truck, and she waved as they left, but she wouldn't be staying at home and catching up on sleep or her chores. Bev had work to do.

She needed a priest.

The Other had called itself a demon. She didn't know what it was, only that it had nested itself into Don, dug in like a tick, intractable. She could do nothing to affect it, other than by killing Don.

But she'd seen The Exorcist and knew of the various myths around possession. She had never believed it was real. It was absurd. She'd spent her whole life examining and analyzing fiction, and that's what all those possession stories were. They were stories, crafted to explain away mental illness, or abuse, or outright fraud. They weren't real. All they were was good fiction.

Until she found herself in one of those stories, and realized that there was no other explanation.

A short drive and she found herself at Crestfield's Catholic Church, Our Lady of Temperance, a big building, one of the oldest in town. It had been built just after the university, a response by the church to lay claim to religion in the town, to not surrender it whole hog to the school.

Or maybe people just wanted a church. She didn't know.

Bev hadn't been in a church for a couple years, since the service for their old friend Thomas Rhodes. But it'd been in the Episcopalian Church a few miles away. She'd pass by this church a thousand times, but had never set foot inside. She stood in front of it, staring up at the steeple, and at the big wooden double doors, and then pushed her way inside, the big door swinging easily on its well-oiled hinges.

The smell inside was a little musty, but mostly pleasant, the faint smell of sweet smoke giving the place a feeling of authenticity and importance. It was beautiful inside, with stained glass windows and a soaring ceiling. The Catholics knew how to make an impression, she'd give them that.

On a random Thursday morning, the chapel was empty. It dawned on her that she had no idea how to find the priest. There were a dozen doors leading off the sanctuary. She started trying them, and all of them were locked. She looked around for any signs posted, about the priest's offices, but she found nothing. Bev kept trying doors, and eventually one opened, but it was only to a small room, a meeting room, the lights turned off, and the chairs put away.

"Can I help you?" asked a voice from behind her, and Bev turned to see a middle-aged priest, his white hair trimmed short, his face lined but pleasant.

"Well, yes, Father," said Bev. "I was looking for you."

"Are you—are you a member of the church?" he asked.

"Oh, no," she said. "I'm not. I've never been here before. I mean, I've lived in Crestfield for most of my life, but I'm not Catholic."

"Ooookay," said the priest, a confused look on his face. "I'm still—" He paused. "Why are you here?"

"I need your help with my husband."

"If you're looking for marital counseling, that's normally reserved for members of the church—"

"No, no Father," said Bev. "It's not that. We're happily married. Or we were."

"I still don't understa—"

"I think my husband is possessed, Father," said Bev. "There's something inside of him, that takes control of him. Something evil. I think it's a demon."

The priest stared at her, the confusion not leaving, but shifting, a little wary now.

"Your husband is possessed?"

"I think so," said Bev. "I know, I sound crazy—" Tears welled in the corners of her eyes, and she cried. "Ugh, I'm so tired of crying." She pulled a tissue from her purse and wiped away the tears.

The priest took a deep breath. "Let's go to my office and talk," he said. "I'm Father Kirk."

"I'm Beverly. Beverly Leal," she said.

"Please, follow me," he said. He took out a keyring and slid one of the numerous keys into one of the identical doors, and Bev followed him through it, into a carpeted, beige hallway, and then a turn, and then another, and through an open door into a rather modest office, with a computer sitting on the desk, the walls covered in shelves, filled with books.

"Here," he said, gesturing to one of the worn chairs in front of the desk. "Please sit."

Bev sat down, the tissue still in her hand.

"Why do you think your husband is possessed?" asked Kirk. His tone of voice said that he was trying to be patient with her, but ultimately thought this was a waste of time.

"My husband Don and I have been married for forty years," said Bev.

"Congratulations."

"Thank you," said Bev. "And he's recently been diagnosed with Alzheimer's—"

"I'm—I'm sorry."

"It's okay," said Bev. "Well, it was okay. Then he started acting strange. Something would come over him. Different from his normal symptoms. He's been losing track of time, forgetting things, getting confused, all of what you think of. But this—this is different."

"Different how?"

"This new person wasn't confused at all. It was composed, and able, and—and quite frankly, evil."

"What do you mean, evil?"

"He—it, whatever it is," said Bev. "It delights in pain. It laughed at bombing victims on the news. It enjoys trauma. It knows which words will hurt me the most."

"You sure this isn't just a side effect of his disease?" asked Kirk.

"The doctor said that a shift in personality is possible," said Bev. "Even likely. But even he was taken aback by what I described. He wants to take Don from me, and put him in a home."

"I am very sorry for what's happened to you, Mrs. Leal. But why do you think he is possessed?"

"Because it called itself a demon, Father. Don calls it The Other. Says he can feel it creeping around inside him. It called itself The Usurper. Says it's as old as time. It knows things it shouldn't. When it's in control, Don is stronger than he possibly could be. His voice changes. I am not a superstitious woman, Father. I believe in rationality, and science. But there is nothing out there that describes what's in my husband but a demon from Hell itself."

Father Kirk stared at her, his face plain. Whatever derision hidden inside had vanished. She'd gotten that far, at least.

"I'm—I'm sorry—" he paused, and took a deep breath. "I want to help, I really do, but I'm not equipped to handle anything like that. The Church itself—we stopped performing exorcisms long ago, except in very, very edge cases. I doubt I could get the Bishop to sign off on even an investigation—"

"What am I supposed to do, Father? Isn't this what you're here for? To fight evil? To combat Hell?"

"I'm sorry, Mrs. Leal, I really am," he said. "But it's a lot more complicated than me saying the Lord's Prayer or throwing holy water at your husband—"

Kirk's face looked overwhelmed, and frustrated, and confused, and Bev wanted to scream.

"So you can't help me?" she asked.

"There's nothing I can do," said Kirk. "I would follow your doctor's advice—"

"The doctor wants to take him away from me, Father! He wants to lock him up, away, alone with that thing inside of him! Where he can rot, and be tortured day after day by that demon, with no solace, no peace, until he dies or that monster gets tired of him!"

Bev's voice filled the room, yelling with anger and fury that had been building and building, and she realized it much too late.

"I'm sorry, Father," said Bev. "I'm sorry for bothering

you." She got up, grabbing her purse. She headed for the office door.

"Mrs. Leal, wait," he said.

Bev turned back, stopping at the door.

Father Kirk looked at her with sad eyes. "I—I can't help you. But I've heard of a priest who may. His name is Father Andrew Martin. He's in New York City, in the Bronx." He scribbled something on a piece of paper, and stood up, and handed it to her. "This is his parish. You can contact him there. He's unconventional. Frowned upon. But he might help."

Bev stared at the paper, and then back again at Kirk. "Thank you, Father."

"Good luck, Mrs. Leal, and God be with you."

19

Tim and Don were waiting for her at home when she left the church. They were doing yard work together, Don pushing a lawnmower, with Tim bagging up yard waste behind him. Tim raised a hand in greeting when they saw her pull up the driveway. The note Kirk had given her was in her purse. She couldn't let Don see it. She couldn't let The Other see it.

"What happened to fishing?" asked Bev.

"We got rained out," said Tim. "Got mixed up with my weather report. Decided to just come back and hang out, if that's okay with you."

"Sure," said Bev.

Don released the lawnmower safety and let it turn off, walking over to them.

"I tried to tell him he didn't need to be on leaf duty, but

he insisted."

"I don't really consider yard work, work at all," said Tim. "And it's not raining here. We can have a beer or two after we're done."

"We'll be tooling around out here," said Don, with a smile. Bev looked at him, and smiled back, the smile of the man she loved, the man she had married. No sign of The Other, and she went inside, doing her best to cherish that smile, but the worry still lingered. The Other was there, waiting. It would wait until the worst moment and then strike at her. It would wake her in the middle of the night, or torture poor Don, or say just the right words that cut down to her heart.

The pair of them worked outside, and Bev retreated inside, and jumped onto their computer to look up information on the priest. Kirk had listed only the parish, its address, and the priest's name. Bev went onto their aging desktop and looked for the parish, and found its contact info. But the priest wasn't listed on their website. There was a number. Bev looked outside, checking to see if both Tim and Don were still out there, so they couldn't hear.

She grabbed the phone and called. She'd ask directly for the priest, and see what he would say. Bev took a deep breath.

The phone rang, and rang, and then when to voicemail.

"Hello, you've reached St. Matthew's Parish, 14 Morgan Street, The Bronx, New York, New York. Please leave a message, and we'll get back to you as soon as we can. *BEEP*."

"Hi, my name is Beverly Leal, and I live in Crestfield, Connecticut. I'm calling to speak to Father Martin. My husband—my husband is possessed, and I was told Father Martin could help me. Please contact me at 555-555-5555."

She hung up, feeling helpless. No answer. She didn't know what else to do but wait. She heard the door open downstairs, and she folded up the note and slid it back into her purse, deep into a pocket where no one would look, not even The Other.

Bev went downstairs to find Don there, sweaty.

"Where's Tim?" asked Bev.

"He went home," said Don. "Tiff said she needed help with a spider, and Tim ran. I told him it was fine. We're going to go fishing next week." He looked at her, his eyes gentle. "Are you okay?"

"I'm okay," she said. She took a deep breath. "How are you?"

"A little tired," he said. "But that's to be expected. I feel—I feel like me."

Bev nodded, not wanting to say anything, because The Other lurked. She knew he did. No matter what they said or did, The Other would be there, waiting for her.

His smile faded a bit, but still remained. "I'm going to take a shower," he said. "I love you."

"I love you too," said Bev, the words like clockwork, and she did love Don, love him more than anything, but she didn't feel them like she once did. Don went upstairs and Bev thought to follow him, but instead she sat at the kitchen table, thinking about her plan. She would wait to hear back from the parish in New York. Maybe that priest would help her. For now, she would have to survive. Make sure Don survived. Somehow placate The Other. Keep it occupied long enough so they could find the help they needed.

Don came down from upstairs not too long after, clean, his short hair wet.

They went about their day, following their normal routine. Or what had been their routine, since the diagnosis. Since the appearance of The Other. Its intrusion on their life had mutated that ordinary life, that routine. Its presence changed every part of their day, even when it was dormant.

Little things. How close they sat together on the couch. How Don's small touches made her feel. Things he said, that she would never ever think as anything but innocuous, now she questioned. The Other wasn't subtle, not when it was present, not when it took control. But still, she knew it lurked, and that apprehension, that tension, was always there. No matter how much Don seemed like himself. She knew The Other could appear at any moment.

Meals together. When they cooked, or when they watched Wheel and Jeopardy every night. It wasn't the same, even if she desperately wanted it to be. The Other took up space, the elephant in the room. Neither could see it, but it was there, keeping them apart.

It didn't stop either of them, though. It wasn't the first thing in their marriage that had slipped in and put distance between them. So they kept trying. They stayed to their normal routine and leaned on that to shoulder the burden as this thing slid in and disrupted everything.

The Other didn't appear the rest of the day, and Bev waited, her eyes now routinely examining her husband, waiting for the demon to appear.

Through dinner, through Jeopardy and Wheel, throughout the night, The Other didn't appear. She slept on a razor's edge now, the smallest thing waking her, but she slept through the night.

Still, she waited. They went about their day the next day.

The space of The Other was still there. But he didn't appear. Don was himself. He still struggled with his symptoms, but they were manageable, downright reasonable compared to the hell of The Other. She remembered things for him and guided him when he lost his way. He was still him, though. Still gentle, still funny, even as he struggled.

That evening and night, and so on. She waited for The Other to appear, and it didn't.

Days passed, and Bev waited, but still The Other didn't show. Not even a hint.

This is a trap.

She knew it was. There was no other explanation for it. It was waiting for her to lose focus, and then it would strike. It wanted to build hope in her, it wanted for her to think that it was gone, and then The Other would dash them, and cause as much pain as it possibly could.

So she waited. She didn't let her guard drop. She watched Don, watched him close. And they continued their normal routine.

A week passed, and The Other still didn't appear, and try as she might, Bev started to hope again.

Maybe it's gone.

The thought came to her, unbid, while they watched Wheel one night. It had been a good day. They'd gone and picked blueberries, both her and his hands thoroughly purple by the end of the day. They'd gotten back, and she'd made a blueberry crumble, and then they ate it with ice cream for dinner. Don had been himself all day, showing almost no symptoms.

It had been a good day.

And now, as they sat there, watching their shows, Bev

couldn't help but feel hopeful. That the dark period of The Other was maybe behind them. That maybe, they could put all that awfulness in a box, and put that box in a dark corner, and never, ever open it.

A small piece of her hoped that it was gone. The rest watched, and waited.

But day after day passed, and still The Other didn't appear.

And her hope grew as well. She worried less and less about what Don would do unattended. She took a shower, or ran to the store without worrying about what he would do alone.

The part of her that echoed *this is a trap* grew smaller and smaller. Because if this was a trap, what was it waiting for? For her to completely drop her guard, just to say "boo!"?

Because if it would leave them, for whatever reason, why would it say goodbye? The Other would want them to worry, want *her* to worry about its absence.

And minute after minute, hour after hour, day after day, The Other stayed away. Three weeks went by, and it didn't show. They laid in bed one night, the lights off, both tired after a long day. The hope had grown, grown so large that it almost engulfed the wary part of her.

"Don—" she started. She paused, their fan softly spinning above them. She took a deep breath.

"What is it, darling?"

"Can you still—still feel it?" asked Bev. "Inside?"

Don shifted in bed. "The Other?"

"Yes."

"How long has it been?"

"Three weeks," said Bev. "It hasn't surfaced for three weeks."

Don exhaled, a long exhale, and Bev heard so much in just a breath.

"I haven't felt anything," he said, his gentle voice lilting to her. "That darkness, that chaos. It's just—just gone. I haven't said anything, because I feel like if I say it out loud, it will hear me, and come back."

"Do you think it's gone?" asked Bev.

"I don't know," said Don. "Nothing has changed, Bev. I'm just trying my best. I haven't always been able to tell when it was here, either. But I can see the difference in you."

"What do you mean?" asked Bev.

"I can see it in your smile," said Don. "The difference. When it's real. And when you're just smiling to try and make me feel better."

Bev's heart shook in her chest and she couldn't stop herself, closing the distance she had created in the bed, embracing him, sliding up next to him and holding him close.

The warmth of his body next to her was home, but inside, she waited, waited for The Other to pop up, to show her she was a fool for hoping, to crush her once again, for that horrible voice to bellow in the dark, and laugh at her, and bring up all the bad things it would do.

She waited, but it didn't rise to the surface. It didn't bellow, it didn't bark. Instead, Don embraced her back, holding her close, his nose in her hair, and then he was kissing her forehead, and her scalp, showering her with kisses.

"I've missed it, Bev," he said, and then Bev kissed him on the lips, in the dark, kissed him once, twice, over and over again, real kisses, with love and depth, something they hadn't shared in an eternity. All the pain and trauma they had gone through washed away with those kisses, along with the last lingering doubt that The Other had left. She didn't know if it was true, but she wanted it to be and that was enough right now, and she kissed her husband hard, and she made love to him, the same man she loved when she was 30, and 40, and 50, and she loved now, all at once.

20

"We're here to celebrate and honor two very special people," said Will Thompson, standing at the podium. The crowd was jammed into the assembly hall at the center.

"They've given their time and energy over the years to grow the Math Empowering Kids Learning Center into what it is today, where thousands of children have learned that math is not just an important skill they can master, but one that's both approachable and fun. Without these two, we wouldn't be where we are today. I wouldn't be where I am today, and I'm betting a fair share of the people here are in the same boat. I could talk about them forever, but I don't think we need that. Let's get them up here, Don and Beverly Leal!"

The crowd applauded, and Don and Bev got up from

their seats near the small stage, walking up the few steps and joining Will. Bev felt her face redden. She'd been in front of classrooms her whole life. She didn't know why it felt so strange now.

Will shook both their hands.

"Don and Beverly have been instrumental in the growth of the Learning Center. Without their time, energy, and knowledge, the center would still be floundering. But we have grown, tripling in size. Because of their efforts, we are renaming the center, to the Donald and Beverly Leal Learning Center!"

The crowd applauded again and then stood to their feet. Bev felt her face grow red, and looked at Don. He hadn't told her they were naming it after them, and he smiled sheepishly back at her.

"Please, please, Don, Beverly, speak," said Will.

Don looked at Bev, and she returned it with wide eyes. She hadn't prepared anything, not for this. Why hadn't he told her?

She gestured back to him, for him to take the mic. Don didn't wait, standing at the podium.

"We are honored, both Bev and I, at having our name attached to such a wonderful place. And that is how I would describe it. A place full of wonder. A place that welcomes children of any background or aspiration, and fills them with the love of not just math, but of learning. I know many graduates of the center are in attendance, and as much as tonight is about the new name of the learning center—I want to thank *you*. Because without you, this place full of wonder is just a building. All of you, you took a chance, and let the learning center, and us, into your heart. And I can't thank you enough. Bev?"

He looked to her, and Bev knew she should say something, they named the place after them, but she hadn't done anything—

And then Don stepped aside, and her feet walked her right in front of the microphone. She took a deep breath.

Speak from the heart, Beverly.

"Thank you so much," she said. "I never expected to be honored in such a way. All the kids who came through the learning center—and I see some of you out there, have already talked to you—you're the stars. You're the special ones. I can't believe—" She felt tears well in her eyes, and then Don reached over, and squeezed her hand, and she looked at him, and felt his strength, and he smiled at her, a warm, loving smile. She wiped away the tears. "If this is our legacy, it's a truly honorable one. Thank you."

*

"You knew, didn't you?" asked Bev. They laid in bed, having returned from the party. Don was wiping his face, and turning off the lights in the bathroom.

"Knew what?" asked Don.

"You knew they were naming the learning center after us," said Bev, staring at him.

"Yes," said Don. "Will told me a few weeks ago."

"But you didn't tell me."

"I thought you'd enjoy the surprise," said Don, joining her in bed. He grabbed a book from his nightstand.

"Don't you lie to me, Mr. Leal," said Bev. "You know I hate surprises." She grabbed the book from his hands and placed it face down in his lap. "Why didn't you tell me?"

Don held silent for a moment, and then met her eyes.

"What would you have done if I told you what they were planning? That they were naming the learning center after us?"

"I mean, it's the same reaction I had tonight," said Bev. "I was flattered. Honored. I meant what I said."

Don looked at her and raised an eyebrow. "Now who's lying?"

A small stab of guilt hit Bev in her gut. "What do you mean?" she asked.

Don took her hand, and held it softly. "I didn't say anything, Bev, because I didn't want to give you the chance to say no."

"Why would I—" she started, but then saw the look in Don's eyes. He raised his eyebrows again, a look she knew well after thirty years of marriage, a look they had exchanged with each other many times over the years.

The look said *you sure?*

"I don't doubt that you're honored, darling. I believe you meant what you said. But when Will told me, I knew right away that you wouldn't want your name up there. That you'd want only my name on the building. And I wasn't going to give you the chance. So, maybe it was mean to not tell you, to spring it on you like that. I am sorry if it hurt you. But that building is part of our legacy, and I wasn't going to risk it."

Bev stared at him. "But my name shouldn't be up there—"

"What did I say?"

"But it shouldn't," she said. "I didn't teach at the center. You did. I don't teach math at all. I helped out from time to time, sure, but—"

"But nothing," said Don. "Yes, I taught there. But those kids needed more than someone to give them arithmetic lessons, or make algebra approachable. They needed someone to listen. To care. To spend time with them, not teaching them anything. Just being there with them. And for every minute I was teaching, you did that. Will and the board were unanimous about both of us being included in the name. You said it, darling. It's *our* legacy. And I wouldn't want it any other way."

Bev took a deep breath. "I accept your apology."

"You did a good job up there, on short notice," said Don. "I knew you would. You were always better at thinking on your feet than I was."

Bev felt the corners of her mouth curl up, and Don smiled sheepishly. Bev grabbed the book in his lap and tossed it off the bed.

"Hey, I was—"

She kissed him, and kissed him hard.

21

Hope lived in her heart again.

Bev woke up having slept the whole night, and turned, and Don was still there, sleeping peacefully. She should get up and start her day. Prepare the house for both of them.

But instead, she rolled over and cuddled up next to him, closing her eyes, dozing.

It was what their retirement was supposed to be. Lazy mornings enjoying each other's closeness. Letting the world come to them. No more stress and no more worry.

They woke up together, and Don insisted on making them breakfast. He didn't need reminding of how she liked her eggs, or how she took her coffee, or if she wanted butter or jam on her toast. He moved through the kitchen adeptly, quickly, his hands as quick as ever while preparing his scrambled eggs and when cooking hers over easy.

She smiled at him. He looked at her, confused.

"What's wrong?"

"Nothing's wrong," she said. "I'm just happy. You're yourself again."

"I feel like myself," said Don. "It's kind of incredible."

Don served them and they ate, Don reading the paper.

"Do we have any plans today?" asked Bev. It was Sunday, and normally it was reserved for Don's yard work.

"No, I don't think so," said Don. "I have an idea."

"What's that?"

"We could go to the farmer's market," said Don. "It's been a long time since we headed down there and checked it out."

Since before the diagnosis.

Bev looked to Don. "You think—you think you can handle it? Being out with so many people?"

"Yeah, I think so," said Don. "I feel good today. We might as well, you know. While we still can." He smiled, and picked up their empty plates, rinsing them real quick and throwing them in the dishwasher. "What do you think?"

"Yeah, let's do it," said Bev. They would only have so many good days. So many opportunities, eventually lost to them. The Other was gone, but the disease was still there. They would carve out joy from it while they still had a chance.

They got dressed, and Bev grabbed a couple of reusable bags and they headed to the car. Don stopped before they got in.

"Do you mind—"

"Mind what?" asked Bev.

"Do you mind if I drive?"

He hadn't driven since the diagnosis.

That's not true. He drove that night. The night you've tried to forget—

"I don't think—"

"Bev—I—I feel good today. I don't know how many more chances I'm going to get," said Don. He looked at her, his eyes big, and vulnerable, and she knew she should put her foot down, but she couldn't deny him. She remembered him flipping the eggs. It was a good day. He could do it. It was one time.

"You sure?"

"Yes," he said. "I can do it."

"Okay," she said. "Today."

They got into his car, instead, with Don behind the wheel. Bev dismissed the feelings of worry.

You're only going to get so many of these days, Bev. Take advantage of them. Enjoy them.

Don backed out of the driveway with ease, with the same practiced movement she had seen him use for decades. Don had usually driven. He liked to drive, always had, and she didn't mind. Driving was a chore to her.

The farmer's market was on campus, only a ten-minute trip away. It had been held in the same place for years and years, and used to be a small market for college kids and a few local residents. The last ten years, however, it had blown up, attracting everyone in town, and even some people coming in from neighboring towns, which attracted more vendors, which drew more people.

They had gone less to it over the years, simply due to that fact, but it still was a fun time, especially considering the sheer variety of goods you could find there.

"You okay?" asked Bev.

"I'm good," said Don, his eyes on the road. His hands glided over the steering wheel. He showed no sign of stress or worry. It was a good day.

The ball of anxiety in her stomach lessened. If they were going to enjoy their time left together, at least while Don was still himself, she would have to not worry all the time. Or at least compartmentalize it.

"I'm excited," said Don. "I'm ready for some of that fresh honey they have."

"It is really good," said Bev. "Although it's so expensive."

"It's worth the money," said Don. "Sometimes you have to splurge on the finer things in life."

They approached the farmer's market, and already the crowds were thick, even with the market just opening. The sidewalks were packed, and all the parking was taken. They'd have to circle back around to find somewhere to park.

"I'll go up and around," said Don. They were behind a few cars which were doing the same thing. The market was just ahead of them, in a massive open area between two buildings on campus, a large fountain the only thing in the square. Food trucks were parked on the edge of it, and people wandered in and out as they went to all the vendors. The vendors were lined for hundreds of feet back into the square, and then even past that, out on the grass and sidewalks surrounding it. A traffic cop stood at the edge of the square, waving people to the left, where there was more parking.

Don stopped a half block back, right in the middle of the street, as the cars ahead of him turned to the left.

"What are you going?" asked Bev. "You can't turn around here." Don's hands squeezed the steering wheel.

"Did you really think I was gone, Beverly?" asked Don.

Not Don. The Other. He had waited.

"No, no no," said Bev, reaching over to the steering wheel, trying to take it from him, but she wasn't stronger than Don, and certainly not stronger than The Other, because the wheel stayed firm in his hands, and he turned and looked at her, his eyes dark and hollow and full of evil. She was wrong, she was stupid, it had hidden all this time, it had waited, it knew she would fall for it—

"I told you," said The Other. "You can not get rid of me, Beverly. I am forever." It gunned the accelerator then, the tires screeching on the pavement, and she knew what he was doing now, she should have seen it, she was blinded, and then it laughed, the car filled with his terrible howling laughter, cackling. The policeman waved frantically and then jumped out of the way as the car sped toward the open area of the market, and Bev reached for the horn and it was too late.

The car thumped against a stall, and then someone bounced off the hood, and she felt a terrible noise as the car ran over something—

Someone

And it only laughed and laughed, his foot never off the accelerator, more people bouncing off the hood, more things thumping underneath, and Bev screamed, until it hit the fountain, and their airbags popped, and even then, it laughed.

*

Bev told the police what they would believe.

Don had lost control of the vehicle, and accidentally hit the accelerator instead of the brake, and killed four people, with dozens more injured.

They released him into her care, but took his license away. Don himself was confused and unsure after the crash. The sure and able Don she had been with was gone. Had he been a product of The Other? Had it orchestrated it all? Had it manipulated her, letting out Don, boosting his capabilities?

She didn't know. Four more people were dead, and there was nothing inside her anymore. Don didn't know what was going on, confused, lost, and she guided him after they went home, returning to a normal routine. The police told her not to let him leave the house, and expect to hear from the district attorney.

The call came the next day, in the afternoon.

"Mrs. Leal?" asked the voice on the other end of the line.

"Yes, speaking," she said.

"This is the Crestfield District Attorney, Daniel Evans."

"Yes," said Bev. "I was expecting your call."

She heard Daniel take a deep breath. "I was informed your husband had been diagnosed with Alzheimer's."

"Yes," she said. "It had been a good day for him, it shouldn't—"

"Mrs. Leal, please," he said. "There are four people dead, and more wounded. That's four cases of vehicular manslaughter, and in most cases similar to this, the jury has come back with guilty charges. It won't be a tough case to prove."

"Oh God," said Bev. Tears poured down her face, and she tried to wipe them away, but there were too many, and she couldn't stop them, no matter what. She was tired of crying, tired of so much pain.

"I don't want to press charges, Mrs. Leal," said Evans. "Considering the mental state of your husband, I don't want to push that cost onto the state, or the cost of a trial—"

"Oh, thank God—"

"But," said Evans. "That's contingent on you surrendering control of him. If you release control of him to a care facility."

Bev's heart dropped, her whole body cold.

"You can't handle him, Mrs. Leal," said Evans. "That's clear. And I won't risk more injuries or death in case he gets behind the wheel again."

"I can't let him go, Mr. Evans," said Bev. "He's my husband! He's my whole life—"

"If you don't surrender him, I will press charges, and he will go to trial, and then he will be taken from you, and placed in a prison with medical care. And the care will not be as good as he would receive in a private facility. I can guarantee you that," said Evans. He took another deep breath. "I'm doing what I can, Mrs. Leal. These people's families will want answers. You should prepare yourself for civil cases. Putting him into a long-term care facility might help your case."

"I—"

"I'll give you a week, Mrs. Leal," said Evans. "Then I need a decision. Goodbye."

*

"Where are we going?" asked Don. The week had passed,

and he hadn't returned to near the state he had been in the morning of the crash. That Don was lost somewhere deep inside.

"Somewhere that will help you," said Bev. "Somewhere where people can take care of you."

"Oh," said Don, looking out the window. The Other hadn't reared his head in the interim, either. Did it get tired, after its appearances? Or was it simply waiting, underneath the surface?

The care facility was an hour's drive away. She had done her research, and it was the best she could afford with their insurance and their savings.

Sadness had overwhelmed her the entire week, and she had reverted back to her routine of keeping an eagle eye on Don, in case The Other came back. But she was mired in sorrow. Over the death of those people, over her guilt, and over losing her husband.

Because the DA was right. She had tried to tell Don about her decision, about what had happened, but he was incapable of having a conversation. She called and talked to Dr. Baumann. He had taken the news hard. He had told her it was rare for cases to advance this quickly.

Not all cases involve demons, Doctor.

They arrived at the facility, which seemed innocuous enough. No gates, no guard. Only a short wall. There were video cameras, though.

She waited while they did a short examination of him, and a consultation with her. It was all double checking, another formality, and every step killed her. Every step another confirmation of her failure as a wife.

And then it was time to say goodbye. They had the room

to themselves.

"I'm going to go," said Bev. "They'll take care of you, okay?"

"Okay," said Don, nodding. His eyes were his, but confused. She hugged him, and she felt tears again, the sorrow overwhelming her, and she forced them away. She couldn't burden them on Don. It would just upset him.

"I am just getting started, Beverly," said The Other, and Bev fell backward, away from Don, and Don's eyes were his. She couldn't breathe, she couldn't breathe, and then she forced breath in. Don was only confused, and now she felt something different from the sorrow and guilt that had overwhelmed her for the past week.

She felt anger.

No.

Not anger.

Rage.

A deep, awful rage at this thing that had taken her husband. As she left the facility, Bev only knew one thing.

She wouldn't let The Other have her husband. No matter the cost.

22

New York City overwhelmed her. She had been once, when she was a kid, but that had been on a field trip, with the entire experience guided.

It was crowded, and noisy, and so, so *big*. She had always avoided big cities, and leaned on Don whenever they had traveled to navigate those enormous spaces. Without him, she had no one to do it but herself.

No one from the parish ever contacted her after multiple phone calls and e-mails, and she didn't know what else to do but go down there herself and knock on the door. She'd need to talk to Father Martin face to face, anyway. She let her anger drive her. Every moment was a moment where Don was locked up, with The Other inside him, doing what it wished. She didn't waste time, and she was in a hotel in New York

City not a week later.

The city was a maze, and once inside her hotel room, she didn't want to leave. But she needed to. The parish wouldn't respond to her, for whatever reason. Bev would go there and get one from them.

Bev left her hotel and flagged a taxi down outside. She knew about Uber and Lyft, but navigating the apps only added stress to her. She'd rather deal with a technology she could handle, which was talking to a person. The taxi got her to the parish, a huge church in the Bronx, which looked at least a hundred years old.

She poked her head inside, and was staggered by the beauty of the old building. The ceiling was fifty feet above her, with beautiful architecture, and stained glass in every window, with huge chandeliers hanging. She understood this. It felt like God belonged here.

She needed to find a priest, or someone. The lobby led off into hallways, and she looked for anyone to talk to. A lot of closed doors, just like the church in Crestfield. Bev sighed and walked down the hallway, looking for anyone. She heard talking from down the hall, and looked inside to see an office with two desks, with a woman sitting at each. They both went silent after she ducked a head in.

Both of the women were dressed professionally, both middle-aged, one slightly older than the other, with silver tinged hair. The other, a brunette.

"Can I help you?" asked the older of the two.

"I hope so," said Bev. "I've left several messages on your voicemail system, and sent multiple e-mails, but I've gotten no responses—"

"What's your name?" asked the older woman.

"Beverly Leal," said Bev. "Is it possible for me to speak to a priest? I was told I could be helped here—"

"Are you a member of the church?" asked the woman.

"No," said Bev.

"Well, do you have an appointment with one of our priests? They're typically very busy, and don't see anyone without an appointment."

"I just told you I haven't gotten any response, from anyone," said Bev. "I needed to talk to someone about an exorcism. I was told Father Martin could help me."

The two women exchanged a quick knowing glance, sharing something that Bev couldn't read, but then the older woman turned back to her.

"I'm sorry, ma'am," she said. "I apologize no one has returned your calls, but Father Martin isn't a part of our parish anymore."

"What do you mean?" asked Bev. "I drove two and a half hours into the city so I could talk to him—"

"He's no longer a part of the parish," she said. "If you wish, I can arrange an appointment with one of our priests, who can talk to you. But they're booked for several weeks—"

"I came to the church for help, but you can't help me for weeks?" asked Bev. "I need help today, not two weeks from now."

"Ma'am, Father Martin is no longer a member of this parish, and I'm unable to give you any more information than that," she said. "One of our other priests may help you more, but all I can do—"

"Yes, I know," said Bev. "Kick me down the road, so I'm a problem in two weeks, instead of today. Thanks for nothing."

She turned and walked out the way she came, glancing once into the massive cathedral, the home of the God that couldn't help her, and she left, leaving the church, going back out onto the street. Traffic flowed by, relatively quiet in the middle of the day.

Father Martin wasn't a part of the parish anymore. She had driven two and a half hours for nothing. Where the hell could he be? Why wasn't he a part of the parish anymore?

She looked up and down the street for a taxi. Bev would go back to her hotel and regroup. Maybe call around to the other churches in the area. Maybe he had switched parishes.

"Ma'am? Ma'am?" asked a voice, and Bev looked instinctively at a woman coming down the stairs from the church. It was the brunette from the office, the quiet one.

"Yes?" asked Bev. "Did an appointment open up? Let me guess, it's six weeks from now, and I'll have to fill out a form in triplicate—"

"No, ma'am," she said, her eyes looking around. "I know where Father Martin is. I—I thought I could at least give you that."

"Why he isn't here?" asked Bev.

"There was some unpleasantness," said the woman. "I can't say anymore. He'll be able to tell you." She held a small piece of paper, hastily ripped from a notepad. She handed it to Bev. "Here, his number and address."

"Address? His home address?" asked Bev.

"Yes," she said.

"He won't mind me having this?"

"He'd probably hate me for giving it out," said the woman. "But he's not here, so he'll have to deal with it. If you need his help, you should have it."

"How far is this from here?"

"Not far," said the woman. She gave Bev directions. "It's probably a fifteen-minute walk."

"Thank you," said Bev. The woman nodded quickly and retreated inside.

Bev followed the woman's directions as best she could, but she got turned around twice, and it took her nearly a half hour to get to the nondescript apartment building. She was sweating, and breathing hard, not used to walking so much in the heat of the city. There was a call box, and the apartment number that should have been the priest's was blank. Bev pushed it anyway.

"Hello?" replied a male voice. It was a start.

"I'm looking for a Father Martin," said Bev.

"He's not here," said the voice.

"Do you know when he'll be back?"

"Go away."

Bev pushed the button again.

"I said go away. Stop bothering me."

"I need to speak to Father Martin," said Bev, again, her voice firm.

"I'm not involved with the parish anymore. Leave me alone," said the voice.

It was him.

He didn't want company? Too bad. Bev waited downstairs, and soon enough a delivery person came through, pushed a button, and someone buzzed them in. She followed the delivery person in and gave them her nicest old lady smile. They smiled back. It always worked.

She wouldn't take no for an answer, not after driving into the city and getting a hotel. Bev imagined Don alone in that facility, alone with The Other, and it pulled up all the moxie she needed. She walked up the stairs to the third floor, to apartment 3C, Father Martin's.

Bev walked to the door, and knocked hard. Three raps. No response.

She knocked again, four hard raps, in quick succession. She heard footsteps walk over to the door, and then silence. Her eyes went to the peephole.

"Father Martin, please, I need to talk to you," said Bev, looking at the peephole.

"Go away," said Martin, from the other side of the door. "Leave me alone."

"Please, Father, I traveled two and a half hours to get here. The priest in my local church told me you were the man to see. That you could—"

"Help you with an exorcism, I know," he said, from the other side of the door. "It seems every priest in the US has heard my name, and thinks I can help every single one of their parishioners that thinks someone they know is possessed. Well, guess what? You're one in a long line of people who have paraded through the parish, and after a while, the bishop got tired of it, and transferred me to California, where I don't want to live, but where I'm headed, anyway."

"I'm sorry, Father, but my husband, there is something inside of him," said Bev. "He's suddenly acting awful. His whole personality changes."

"And let me guess, he's recently been diagnosed with dementia? Or borderline personality disorder? Or schizophrenia? Or some other disease of the mind?"

"Well, yes—"

"Exactly," said Martin, almost shouting on the other side

of the door. "I believe in demons, but it doesn't mean I don't believe in mental health. And they're not the same thing. I wish the other priests could understand the difference before pointing every single person with a problem my way. Please, ma'am, I'm sorry about your husband, but leave me alone. I'm packing. I have to be out of here by tomorrow."

"Father Martin," she said, her head up against the door. "Please, listen. Yes, he's been diagnosed with Alzheimer's. But the demon, it said itself, that's how it got inside him. It said it made it easy to slip right in. My husband called it The Other. He says he can feel it inside, but can never see it. It's invisible. It's—it's killed five people, Father. It called itself The Usurper."

There was a small sound from the other side of the door.

"What did you say?" asked Martin, his voice barely audible.

"I said it called itself The Usurper. It came out, and talked to me. Threatened me and my husband. Held us hostage. Knows things my husband couldn't know. Makes him stronger than he could possibly be. Please, please help me, if you can. You're all I have left."

There was silence from the other side of the door that stretched forever. Bev leaned back off the door, took a deep breath.

Nothing.

She went to leave, and then the door opened. A young man stood on the other side, dressed in basketball shorts and a white tank top, his short brown hair slightly tousled. He looked tired.

"I'm sorry, ma'am, for my rudeness. Please come inside. We should talk."

23

Father Martin pulled out two folding chairs, his small apartment crammed from wall to wall with boxes.

"I'm sorry, this is all I have," he said. "I have to have all this stuff on a truck tomorrow."

"A seat's a seat," said Bev.

"I am sorry for my rudeness," said Martin. "I've—I've had a trying time."

"I see that," said Bev. "I'm just happy to talk to someone. Everyone's been giving me the runaround. The church wouldn't return my messages or my emails, and one of the woman working in the office acted like giving me your information was like we were in the French Underground."

"I—I had a falling out with the parish," said Martin. "I showed my ass, so to speak."

Bev laughed. She hadn't laughed in days, and just the sensation made her feel better. "I'm sorry for laughing."

"No, it's okay," said Martin. "It was quite ridiculous. Enough about me. Please tell me about your husband."

Bev told him, starting with the anniversary party, and ending with them crashing into the crowd at the farmer's market, with The Other laughing as he killed strangers. Father Martin only listened, his eyes closed, his hands clasped. Bev took him on his word and continued to speak, even as the words were hard, and she struggled. She didn't cry, however. She had promised herself that she wouldn't cry, not anymore.

"And then I came to see you," said Bev. "Because Don is still in the care facility, but so is The Other, trapped in there with him. I shouldn't say trapped, because I think it can leave at any time. But it enjoys tormenting him. I'll do anything, Father. Whatever it takes."

The small apartment was quiet for a moment, and outside sounds filtered in, from the street and neighboring apartments.

"You said the demon had killed five," said Father Martin, finally. "Who was the fifth?"

Bev took a deep breath. "No one knows about it but me. It was the first. It crept from our bed in the night, and slaughtered a homeless man. At random. I followed it, and saw. When I confronted Don about it, that's when The Other emerged. It threatened to kill Don if I went to the police."

Father Martin stared at her, his mouth closed tight, his eyes grim and distant.

"You said it called itself The Usurper?"

"Yes," said Bev. "It said it had many names over the years.

But most called it The Usurper. It said it would add The Other to its list."

Father Martin took a deep breath and let it out slowly.

"What is it, Father?" asked Bev. "Do you know that name?"

"Yes," said Martin. "I've encountered the name before in my studies. And I've encountered the demon before, if indirectly."

"Your studies?"

"Yes," said Martin. "The Catholic Church doesn't publicize its history with demons, but there is one. Before the age of science, when the presence of demons was more accepted, it wasn't nearly as secretive. But now—now it only wants us to see demons as metaphors. As stand-ins for someone's struggle with alcoholism, or with anger, or lust. But demons are real. They exist in our world, spreading disorder, chaos, and pain."

"Where do they come from? Hell?"

"That word is probably the easiest to use, if you wish to describe their origin," said Martin. "But I don't think it's as simple as that. Catholicism describes Hell as eternal hellfire, devoid of the grace of eternal life. About the punishment of sinners, etc. I've read everything the Church has written about Hell, and most of it is made up, quite frankly. And I understand the impulse. But I don't wish to describe Hell in poetic metaphor. I want concrete information. Because I believe Hell exists, Mrs. Leal. I believe that Lucifer exists there, and that The Usurper, among others, sprang from it. But I don't know what it is. I haven't been there, and no one else has either, at least not anyone that's returned. And certain people in the Church find my views heretical."

"You've encountered The Other before?"

"Only indirectly," said Father Martin. "After the fact. But you saying its name froze me. Because I have cleaned up after its carnage."

"Carnage? What happened?"

"It was a bomb," said Martin. "It didn't seem that, on the surface. It was ruled a terrible accident. It killed quite a few people. I was called in by one of the few remaining family members."

"What did it do?"

"After I investigated, it became clear that it was a car bomb. The Usurper—The Other—had possessed a man, and after tormenting his family for a time, he turned his car into a bomb, and blew it up outside of a minor league baseball game. It killed a dozen people, including the man who was possessed. But it was ruled an accident by an ad-dled man. The family contacted me after my name got to them through the grapevine, and they had a similar story to yours. An aged family member, his behavior sudden-ly changing, suddenly becoming antagonistic, becoming *mean*. They knew something was wrong. Only one of them had spoken to it. It also had called itself The Usurper. Un-fortunately, when I returned to the parish is when the un-pleasantness started, and most of my resources were taken from me. I didn't get to dig into any research. I had hoped, perhaps foolishly, that it had perished along with its victim in the blast. That it would be cast back down to Hell. I was wrong to hope. It jumped out before the bomb went off, and wandered until it found another victim."

"It told me that if it ever killed Don, it would leap out before it happened. That Don alone would be a victim."

Father Martin considered her for a moment, and then nodded. "That likely confirms what I believed. It is able to leave at will, but is vulnerable while still in the victim's body."

"What can we do, Father?" she asked.

"I don't know," said Father Martin. "I've never encountered a demon in the wild."

"What does that mean?"

"It means that I've never met one, face to face," said Martin. "They're incredibly shifty. You told me it bragged about being invisible. About being able to leap out of Don at the first sign of trouble. Despite all of their knowledge and craftiness, they are still only able to affect the world while in a mortal body. And even then, it seems The Other can only slide into those suffering from a sort of mental disability, or disease. The few others I've found evidence of—they like staying in the shadows. They prefer the Church to ignore them, to treat them in the abstract. They don't want to be confronted."

"We need to do something," said Bev.

"We'll need to figure that out," said Martin. "But I'm in a rough spot right now."

"What's that?" asked Bev.

"Everything I own is being put on a truck tomorrow, and then I'm getting on a cross-country train to California. The Church is expecting me in Sacramento in a few days. Until recently, they had been funding my trips to investigate these occurrences. But now, I don't have any money. I don't have a car."

"I have a car."

"We may need more than that, depending on what and where we need to research. It may get expensive."

"I have money. I have our retirement fund."

"You shouldn't—"

"Father, we built up that money with the idea we'd spend the last years of our life traveling and seeing the world. That dream is dead. I might as well use the money destroying the thing that killed it."

Martin held her stare for a moment, and then grimly nodded.

"Will the Church be upset when you don't show up on time to Sacramento?"

"Oh, certainly," said Martin. "Especially after all the yelling I did at the bishop here. But I believe it's better to ask for forgiveness than for permission."

"Well, what's the next step?"

"Mrs. Leal—"

"Please, call me Bev."

"Bev," said Father Martin. "Before we do anything, I—I don't want you to be misled about our chances."

"They said you're an expert."

"I'm about as close as they come in the modern Church," said Martin. "And that's why I know it's still highly unlikely we find anything of use. Or find anything that can potentially drive out or kill The Other. They're tenacious, otherworldly things. If I told you we were going into combat with an angel, would you expect to win?"

Bev stared. "No."

"And while they are certainly not the same thing, they are both uncontrollable servants of a greater thing. The forces needed to combat them are sometimes just beyond human reckoning."

"Are you saying we'll need the hand of God to stop The

Other?"

"No," said Martin. "I'm saying that whatever may stop The Other, is impossible for us to reckon with. No matter how much money or intelligence, or courage we push with, it still won't matter. Some things are out of our control. It is the nature of fighting demons. Sometimes you can have everything swing in your favor, and still lose. You said your husband is currently in a care facility. Locked up."

"It's not a maximum security prison," said Bev. "But he can't leave, not without my say so."

"I'll tell you now, so you're ready," said Martin. "Because we may spend a great deal of time and money, and in the end, decide that he's better off right there. That while he's locked up, The Other has a very limited sphere of influence. And certainly, he may hurt your husband, and perhaps some others in the facility. But the rest of the world is safe while he's in there."

Bev couldn't stop the tears then, no matter how she tried to force them back down. She ruffled through her purse, looking for tissues. Father Martin pulled a box from an empty bookshelf and placed them in front of her.

"I'm sorry, but it had to be said before you commit more resources."

"No, I understand," said Bev. "But I want you to understand. That thing has control of my husband, and is almost certainly spending what energy it can muster to make his life a living hell, along with whoever is in the facility with him. My husband has Alzheimer's, and I honestly don't know how much more time he has, even without that monster's influence. But I *will not* have my husband's last days spent with that thing. If he dies, he does not die alone with his last moments spent with that monster. I don't care what it takes. It said—it said that it was our love that makes Don so attractive. That it feeds on the pain caused by damaging that love." She stared at Father Martin, her eyes now hard. "I will show it what damage love can cause when sharpened into a sword."

Father Martin nodded. "That's what I needed to hear. Then let's start."

"What's the first step?" asked Bev.

"I need to talk to it."

24

Two days later, they stood at the entrance to the care facility. Bev felt focused this time, keeping her sadness and sorrow at arm's length. They had a mission today, and that was to talk to The Other.

For so long, she had done her best to keep that thing away. Today, they would do their best to find it. Bev had questioned if Father Martin truly needed to speak to it, if it wasn't a better idea to leave the demon in the dark as to his involvement. But he insisted.

"There are very few opportunities to interrogate a demon directly. I can't pass up this chance. We need all the intelligence we can get before we move on to the next steps."

And so they went into the facility. The administrator had balked at Bev visiting so quickly after dropping off Don, but the mention of a priest accompanying her had smoothed out her request. They snaked their way through the facility, past the checkpoints, past all the attendants. She noticed now which ones carried billy clubs, and which were unarmed, and which of the checkpoints were manned, and which weren't.

After a few minutes of walking through identical tiled hallways, led by a nurse, they found themselves in Don's room, which contained a bed, a modest sitting area, a small flat screen television, and a bathroom. There was also a mini-fridge, a microwave, and a kitchen sink, if he wanted to eat away from the cafeteria. They were left alone with him, after the nurse showed them where the alert button was, if they needed anything.

Don smiled when he saw Bev, standing up and embracing her. He seemed a little more cogent than when she dropped him off.

"Don, this is Father Martin," said Bev. "Father, this is my husband, Don."

Don extended a hand, shaking the Father's.

"Nice to meet you, Father," said Don, but Don's face was full of confusion. "I don't mean to be rude, Bev, but why did you bring a Catholic priest?"

Bev studied his face, not sure what Don meant. "He's here to talk to The Other. We're going to try to help."

Don looked back with bewilderment. "What do you mean, The Other?"

"You told me about it, honey," said Bev. "You said you could feel it inside. Father Martin can help with it."

"The doctors, the doctors said that it's not real," said Don. "That I shouldn't talk about it like it's real."

Bev exchanged a quick glance with Father Martin, who shot her a glance back. He stepped forward.

"It's nice to meet you, Don," said Father Martin. "Your wife loves you a lot, and that's why I've come to help you. Despite what the doctors might say, The Other is absolutely real. And you'll have to forgive me, but it's the one I'm interested in speaking to. So if it's in there, I'd like to speak to The Other now."

Don glared at him with confusion. "Young man, I—"

Father Martin stared at him, and his voice changed, a hard edge that Bev hadn't heard from him. "Demon, you may think you've hidden from God's sight, but we see you. And now I call upon you with the name of God."

"Son—"

"I don't want to talk to Don Leal, I want to talk to The Other. In God's name, I summon it."

"I can't help, Father," said Don. "I don't want that part of me—"

"It's not a part of you," said Father Martin. "And no matter how much it wishes to hide, it can't hide under God's light. Reveal yourself now, Usurper!"

Don flinched at the last word, and he stared at Father Martin, stationary and still, not saying anything. His eyes shifted as he stared, and Bev saw The Other emerge, Don's mouth widening into an impossible grin, and then the same braying laughter from the day of the crash emerged, filling Don's room.

It laughed, loud and hard, doubling over as it shrieked, before standing up and sitting in Don's recliner, popping the footrest up with a casual motion.

"Beverly," it said, the same deep and steady voice as before, so different from Don's. "I see you have brought me a new friend. A holy man. God does not summon me, and he has no power over—"

"You're speaking to me, and not to her," said Father Martin, his voice hard now, commanding attention. The Other's eyes went to Martin, with venom.

"Oh, is that a fact?" asked The Other.

"It's a fact," said Father Martin. "You're speaking to a messenger of the Lord, and I demand respect."

The Other laughed again, lounging back in Don's recliner.

"Respect?" asked The Other. "What a laughable ideal. Let me correct myself. A *boy*, dressed in holy garb. Disguised in authority. You have seen the Earth so little, boy, and you pretend to represent the One Above? How foolish of you."

Father Martin stood firm, matching the glare of The Other.

"Well, you wanted to speak. Here I am. Speak."

"I command you to leave the body of Don Leal, and never return. I command you to return to Hell, and leave Earth forever," boomed Father Martin.

The Other only stared at him, his grin still there, but didn't smile.

"No," said The Other.

"You deny the request?" asked Father Martin.

"Yes, I deny the request," said The Other. "Such formality. But it has been quite an age since I have encountered anyone that knows the ritual."

"I'm not a young priest, pulled off the street," said Martin.

"No, I suppose not," said The Other. "But it does not

matter. You can do nothing to me, just like the doctors. Just like her. I am invincible, invulnerable, in this form."

"That is not true."

"Is it not?" asked The Other. "Then compel me. Stop dancing with your silly words, that have not worked on one of my kind in five centuries. Use your Lord's power, to pull me out."

Father Martin did nothing.

"See?" said The Other. "You have no power over me. And even if you are familiar with the form, and the ritual, they both mean nothing in this day and age. Your Church has forgotten about me, and with its amnesia, you have no strength."

"That is not true," said Father Martin. "There are still ways. Why do you stay with this man? You are under lock and key now. You could leave him, and go find someone more fruitful."

"Ah, you are wrong again, boy," said The Other. "Because this form bears *so much fruit*. It is a delicious peach, juicy, and dripping every day, every hour, every moment." The Other licked his lips, and Bev forced herself not to charge over and shake it, to try to shake it loose from her husband. "You could not know, boy. You are too young. Because this fruit takes time to grow, more time than you have had. Their love, holy child, is so rich. Why would I abandon such a sumptuous feast?"

"You thrive on pain, on chaos," said Father Martin. "You can't cause much, in here."

"Do you ever grow weary of your assumptions?" asked The Other. "Because my reach is far, even here, locked away with the feeble and dying. Farther than you could fathom."

"Is that a fact?" asked Father Martin.

"Yes," said The Other. "And why does that matter, anyway, holy child? I have an eternity here. I can dawdle when I wish, linger, and enjoy the fruit of decades of affection and devotion, as I feel the torment of this man, deprived of his love."

"You monster!" yelled Bev. She couldn't stop herself, and she charged him then, and then Father Martin was there, holding her, rage filling her.

"I know it's hard, Bev, but let him speak," said Martin, a whisper in her ear, and all the while the dark eyes of The Other considered her, gleefully.

"See her passion? See her *indignation*? All driven by such abiding love, built over years and years. These humans, they live such short lives, but their love is so deep, so boundless. When you sever that relationship, mhmm. It is so deeply satisfying. So *filling*."

"Please, Bev," said Father Martin. "I have this in control." Bev looked to him, and his eyes were confident, the young priest who looked lost two days ago now looking sure.

She blinked and then turned away, and sat on Don's bed, and she could smell him there, and it soothed her enough. Father Martin turned back to The Other.

"I'm glad that we could finally meet," said Father Martin. "I've been on your trail."

"Oh, is that right?" asked The Other. He smiled wide again.

"Yes," said Father Martin. "The bombing. I had investigated it, on behest of the family. That's where I first heard your name. When you killed John Braddock, and all those other people at the baseball game."

"Yes," said The Other. "I had a lot of fun with John, but like all of my toys, it came to an end. An explosive one."

"Yes, it was quite a tragedy," said Father Martin. "But I would like to tell you they've recovered quite well. Both the family and the baseball team. It was an affiliate of the Dodgers, and the owner made a substantial donation in tribute to John Braddock, and everyone else that died there. The family used the insurance money to start a non-profit of their own. In the end, a lot of good was done in his name."

"I do not care about that," said The Other, and his smile was gone. Bev watched.

He does know what he's doing.

"I think you do," said Father Martin. "Because you've already mentioned how much enjoyment you get from causing pain and suffering. And how much more enjoyable it is when there's so much deep love that you're inflicting damage upon. But, here's the thing. However much pain you cause in the immediate, is overtaken by the recuperative powers of humanity."

"You are speaking rubbish—" The Other didn't recline any more, sitting on the edge of the chair.

"No, I'm not," said Father Martin. "Humanity is God's greatest creation, because of that ability to heal. To look at something that's awful, and damaging, and painful, and to use that energy to create something helpful, and recuperative, and loving."

"Stop it—"

"And that's just in that one instance," said Father Martin. "Now, I certainly haven't tracked down every single one of your incarnations, but of all the ones I've found, certainly there's been trauma, and pain, but all of it is superseded by heart and healing. Every single time you've arrived, you've set off a bomb, sometimes literally. But also, every single time, the people you've left behind have picked up the pieces, and built something bigger, and better, and something that will help more people in the long run."

"That is nonsense, you are lying—"

"Despite your intentions, everywhere you've gone you've seeded hope. Despite your evil, you've created only good."

"Shut up, shut up, shut up! I am darkness. I am evil incarnate. I devour hope and love. You want me out of this body? It will never happen, never! I will only flee when Don breathes his final breath!" The Other snarled every word, and then the sounds coming from his throat weren't words at all, at least not in any human language. Father Martin stood his ground, even as Bev saw blood trickle from his ears. The Other frothed now, as those terrible noises emerged, and then he shook, his teeth rattling in his mouth.

"Press the call button, Bev," said Father Martin, his eyes staying on The Other, and then it was only Don, shaking, and soon nurses came into the room, and saw him, and called for more help.

25

Nurses came in and sedated Don, and Bev wanted to stay, to help, but she and Father Martin were ushered away, and then politely told to come back another day.

"What was that?" asked Bev, sitting in her car. "Are you okay?" Father Martin had a tissue, and was wiping away the blood that had dried underneath his ears.

"I'll survive," said Father Martin. "The Other lost control."

"Lost control?"

"Yes," said Father Martin. "Despite the appearances, it takes a lot of effort from these demons to keep control of a human host. I wanted to know how strong it is."

"And?"

"It's relatively powerful," said Martin. "It denied my

request as a servant of God, which makes it something to reckon with. It dismissed it, even. I disrupted its hold on Don, though. It's not invincible."

"Are your ears okay?"

"They will be."

"How did it do that?"

"If you want proof, concrete proof, that this is a demon, and not just Don's personality shifting, this is it. Demons have power beyond just possessing people. If they focus hard enough, with their hate, with their rage, then they can cause nervous system disruption in others."

"Nervous system disruption?" asked Bev. "How far can they go?"

"Are you asking if they can kill someone?" asked Martin. "Because yes, possibly, but only the most powerful demons. It also requires a lot of focus, a lot of effort. I believe that was the most The Other can do. At least externally. I wanted to test its power. Now we know."

"Did that hurt Don?"

"No more than usual," said Father Martin. "I apologize for not giving you warning. But I couldn't give away my plan. But now I have a better sense of what we're dealing with. And I know it's The Usurper."

Bev stared ahead at the care facility, with Don somewhere inside, sedated after their encounter. "What's next?"

Father Martin stared ahead as well. "I have some good news, and some bad news."

"I'll take the good news first," said Bev.

"I know what the next step is," said Father Martin. "I know what we need, to get more information on The Other. Maybe even how to exorcise it."

"What's the catch?" asked Bev. "What's the bad news?"

"The bad news is it's in the Vatican."

"In Italy?"

"Yes," said Father Martin. "The Church has a vast library of books and tomes on demonology. They would never admit to such, of course, but they exist. When I'd encountered The Other before, I'd done some preliminary investigation. I have a friend there, and he did a little digging. There's a book there with some information on The Usurper, on The Other. If I can get my hands on it, we may find the secret to The Usurper, and cast him out of Don."

"Italy isn't exactly right next door."

"No."

"Is there no way for us to access this book here? Or have someone else read it?"

"These are not normal books," said Father Martin. "The Church keeps them only because they cannot be destroyed."

"What do you mean, can't be destroyed?"

"They are indestructible," said Father Martin. "Literally. The pages can't be burned, or ripped. The books cannot be torn apart or damaged. They are intrinsic. And frankly, the Church really doesn't want anyone reading them."

"Why not?"

"How do you think The Other came to Earth in the first place?" asked Father Martin. "The book that will tell us that is the same book that will tell us how to excise him. But any one of those books contains terrible knowledge that could spell Hell on Earth."

"But you can get access to it?"

"Well—probably," said Father Martin. "I am friends with the librarian. And he may let me have some time with the book."

"May?"

"Yes."

"So we'll fly to Rome, and then get into the Vatican, just so you can *maybe* read a book?" asked Bev.

"Again, I believe it is better to ask for forgiveness rather than permission. But when push comes to shove, the Church doesn't want me reading the book. They don't want anyone reading them, even higher officials in the Church, even if they're technically allowed. So if certain someones realize what I'm doing, or that I'm there, they'll try and stop me. Well, they won't try. They'll succeed. They have armed guards. But I don't expect it to come to that. I expect to slip in, find the book I need, find the information we need, and then slip out."

"Is it the only way?"

"The only way I know of," said Father Martin. "These books—they do exist in the wild. Some in the hands of private collectors, with other churches. And still a few more, in the hands of those who wish to use them."

"To summon demons?"

"Yes," said Father Martin. "It's why—" He stopped.

"Why what?" asked Bev.

"It doesn't matter," said Martin. "We need to get to Rome."

"Then Rome it is," said Bev. "I need to find my passport."

*

They were flying over the Atlantic ocean the next day. Bev had flown overseas once, when she was in college. She had gone to London with her sister and mother. That was a lifetime ago.

She stared out the window at the ocean, the field of blue far, far below. They'd been in the air for hours. Father Martin sat next to her, reading on his tablet.

"What are you reading?"

"It's a book about climate change."

"I didn't—"

"You didn't expect a priest to believe in science?"

"No," said Bev. "I just usually reserve lighter reading for planes."

"I find it fascinating," said Father Martin. "It is apocalypse, staring us in the face. I don't turn away from problems, or ignore them. I face them head on. I don't believe in hiding things that are dangerous. Or acting like they don't exist."

"Like the Church?"

"Yes," said Father Martin. "Anything that isn't the right image, or the right branding, is hidden away. Nothing can sully the precious image of the Catholic Church."

"I don't think that's true," said Bev. "After all the abuse scandals—"

"Oh, I know," said Father Martin. "It's disgusting. And the majority saw that and acknowledged the horrible things. But instead of confronting it, the Church tried to ignore it. Put their head in the sand. Who cares if the world sees us as abusers? We must not break ranks, even if we are shoulder to shoulder with monsters."

"How do you—I don't know how to phrase it—"

"How can I still be a member of the Church, knowing what they've done? Knowing, in some cases, what they continue to do?"

"Yes."

"You're not the first person to ask," said Father Martin. "I became a priest because I felt a calling from God. I know that's what everyone says, but it does not make it a lie. And I believe the Church is ultimately a good in the world, and that if I, and many others, continue our work, we can improve it from within, and make it what we want it to be." He paused. "But believe me, there are days where I want to take off my collar and find another way to honor that calling. And lately, those days have come closer and closer together. And maybe, that day will come, when I give up the priesthood."

"And become a full-time demon hunter?"

Martin chuckled. "Is that what you think of me as?" he asked. "A demon hunter?"

"Well, what are you, then?" asked Bev. "You were recommended by a priest, who said you had knowledge about possession. You were kicked out of the parish, and now we're flying to the Vatican for information on fighting demons."

"I'm a servant of God," said Father Martin. "That's how I think of myself. I'm just chasing down things that most people are afraid to acknowledge."

"But why this?" asked Bev. "I imagine it's not a track in seminary school, or something."

"No," said Martin. "I had—had an encounter with a demon at a young age. I didn't know what it was. But with time, and meditation, I realized. And with what it did to me—with how much it affected me, and changed my life—I wanted to stop that happening to other people."

"What happened to you?"

Martin paused.

"I'm sorry—I shouldn't have asked," said Bev. "You don't have to—"

"No, it's okay." He took a breath. "A demon killed my father. It took him from me at a young age. He was—he was a good man, and the demon killed him. If I can stop that from happening—if I can send them back to where they belong, then I will have done my part."

"I'm sorry," said Bev. "I didn't realize."

"No," said Father Martin. "It's important to talk about it. We can't let them dwell in the shadows. We have to drag them into the light. Trying to ignore them has let them operate with impunity. It's led to men like Don getting taken."

Bev took a deep breath and looked out the window. She saw Italy in the distance. They were close. The pilot came over the PA, telling them they'd be beginning their descent soon.

"I've never been to Italy," said Bev. "We were planning a trip—before, before everything."

"It's a beautiful place," said Father Martin. "I don't think we'll have much time for sightseeing, though."

"As long as we find an answer for The Other, I think I'll deal."

The plane started down. Bev watched them descend.

26

"Where are we going?" asked Bev. "Shouldn't we go into the main entrance?"

It was early in the morning, the next day. Father Martin had insisted that they go the next day, and not that night.

"No," said Martin. The early morning sun was rising over the buildings surrounding Vatican City. Bev tried to stay focused on the path ahead, but everywhere she looked was history and beauty, and it was hard not to stare. "There really isn't a 'back way' into Vatican City, but Father Benedetto said he'd be waiting for me at the south gate."

"They wouldn't let you in?" asked Bev.

"They probably would, if I pressed the guards, but just because I'm a priest doesn't mean I can just go wherever I please. Especially if they realize I'm American. I just hope

Michael doesn't forget about me. Wouldn't be the first—"

The streets were already thick with tourists, and Bev imagined it'd only get worse as the day went on. They walked past the massive St. Peter's Square, where hundreds of visitors were already lined up for access to the museum and other attractions inside the city.

They followed the wall surrounding Vatican City to the south, where there was a small gate.

"Oh, thank God, he didn't forget," said Martin. A priest stood to the side of the gate, his head on a swivel. When he saw Father Martin, he let a slim smile loose and did a short wave.

"Andrew," said Father Benedetto, extending a hand. Father Martin grabbed it, and they both shook with two hands. Benedetto had a slight accent, but only slight.

"Michael," said Martin. "It's nice to see you again."

"You as well, Andrew," said Benedetto. He looked to Bev.

"This is Beverly Leal," said Father Martin. Benedetto extended a hand and shook hers, his skin soft.

"Come with me," said Benedetto. "Beverly, I ask that you stay close to us. The public are largely unwelcome unattended within the walls of the city, and the guards will not be shy to escort you away."

Bev nodded and stuck close to both the priests, even as Benedetto moved quickly, first on the open streets of Vatican City, and then into a building, and down a hallway. Bev felt the eyes of other clergy and of Vatican guards as they walked, but no one stopped them. Benedetto and Martin looked like they belonged, and so they accepted the civilian that walked with them.

Father Martin said nothing, only following Father Benedetto through the hallways of different buildings, some ancient, some modern, jumping backward and forward through time as they moved through the grounds.

They ended their journey in a small office, which wouldn't look out of place in an accounting firm. Father Benedetto sat behind the desk, and Martin and Bev took their places in the chairs in front of him.

"We can talk here," said Benedetto. "It's been a long time, Andrew."

"It has," said Father Martin, his face different here, then any other time Bev had seen him. Relaxed, maybe? She couldn't tell. Strange, when they were about to open some unholy tome to find a cure for demon possession.

"How have you been?" asked Benedetto.

"Not great, honestly," said Martin. "My reputation has preceded me, and is starting to overwhelm me."

"I warned you, didn't I?" asked Benedetto. "Why do you think I keep my studies quiet? If the bishops knew, I wouldn't have this office. I'd be out in the wilds somewhere, tending sheep."

"You did," said Father Martin. "But it couldn't be helped. I knew the path I set upon. So—do we have access?"

Benedetto frowned. "You still haven't told me the details."

"I thought you didn't want to know. Plausible deniability."

"You shouldn't tell me, you're right. Because it's healthier for my career not to know, but still—I am curious. What have you encountered? It must be something, for you to come all this way."

Father Martin stared and raised an eyebrow, testing Benedetto. Whatever the test was, he passed. "The Usurper."

"Oh," said Benedetto, frozen still. "The same—"

"Yes," said Father Martin, cutting him off, with a glance to Bev. "It has inhabited Donald Leal, Bev's husband."

"I'm sorry," said Father Benedetto. "I didn't realize."

"We just want a way to remove it," said Bev.

Benedetto's eyes widened for a moment, and twisted his head, holding back words. "So you want to try again with its book?"

"Yes," said Father Martin. "I think—"

"Can you handle it, this time?" asked Benedetto.

"Yes," said Father Martin. "I wouldn't have come this far without the belief."

"You believed before—"

"I was young," said Father Martin. "I can do it now."

"I hope you're right," said Benedetto.

"We can have access, correct?" asked Father Martin.

"Yes," said Benedetto. "But—"

"But what?"

"But I can't run interference for you," said Benedetto. "If I'm not attending my duties, people will notice, and come find me. And then find you. You're on your own. I don't know you're here."

"So—if I get caught, you weren't the one who let me in?" asked Father Martin.

"Correct," said Benedetto. "I have to deny any responsibility. It's a marvel I get access to the forbidden books at all. If they knew I was letting others read them—I *would* be out in the wilderness, tending sheep." He took a pen and scribbled down something on a small piece of paper. "This is the access code for the number pad on the door. Make sure to hit the pound sign at the end. Put everything back when you leave and don't check in with me. I'll text you later."

They shared another glance, that Bev couldn't parse, and then Martin stood up, and shook Benedetto's hand one more time, and then looked at her and they were out the door. Martin walked with purpose, knowing exactly where he was headed.

"People will look at us," said Martin. "Don't make eye contact. Stay right next to me. I apologize for the pace, but time does matter now. There is a clock ticking." Bev nodded, but Martin was already striding forward again, moving through the halls of the building. Bev had no idea where they were in the greater context of Vatican City, but they turned and went through another set of doors, and then another set, and then one more set, and then they came to another door, that looked innocuous, and they went through it, and in front of them was another door, but this had a keypad on it, and Martin pulled the note from his palm and typed in the number, and there was a small beep, and they went inside, and then the door locked behind them.

Martin stopped. They had finally arrived. When Martin had described the archive of forbidden books, indestructible, containing cursed knowledge, she had imagined something dark and musty, bookshelves filled with heavy, leather-bound books that screamed at the touch.

She hadn't imagined this. It looked like the periodical room in the Crestfield library. Shelves lined the walls, filled with books. But it had clean, even lighting. Glass doors covered all the shelves. Two desks stood in the center of the room, facing each other. The floor was beige carpet, the walls off-white. It was boring.

"This wasn't what I expected," said Bev.

"Did you expect demons leaping from pages?" asked Martin.

"I don't know."

"It's still a library, even if the books are dangerous," said Father Martin. "And don't let the looks deceive you. These books *are* very dangerous."

"What was Benedetto talking about? He mentioned you've tried this before?"

"Yes," said Martin. "When I was younger, my first time at the Vatican. Benedetto and I hit it off, and I talked him into letting me investigate The Other's book. It did not end well."

"What happened?"

"I went to the hospital," said Martin. "I had a heart attack."

"Jesus," said Bev. "Oh, sorry."

He waved her off. "I was young, and in over my head. I've done a lot more research, and a lot more work in the meantime. It won't happen again. I'm much more worried about being interrupted by Vatican guards. They will not take kindly to us being in here."

"Well, do you know which book you're looking for?"

"Yes," said Martin. "I can feel it."

"What do you mean?"

"Most of these books are not just books," said Father Martin. "They're not alive, per se, but they definitely are not dead."

"I don't understand," said Bev. "Are you telling me the books are sentient?"

"Not quite," said Father Martin. "As far as we can tell, they have a low degree of—something—coming off them.

Radiation would be a good analogue. A field. Bad energy. We haven't been able to really get a reading, because again, they can't leave this room, and the Church will not have scientists come in here and examine them."

"I don't feel anything," said Bev.

"Well, I've already opened the book once, and read some of it," said Father Martin. "So it has a stronger effect on me. But I think that if you wait, and be quiet, you'll feel it. With this many books, and even with the wards placed by the clergy, you should still feel it."

"Wards?"

"Blessings," said Father Martin. "It helps keep them— calm, I guess would be the word. Otherwise, it'd be foolhardy to keep them all together like this. Just be quiet, close your eyes, and take a couple breaths."

Bev closed her eyes and stood still. She took a deep breath, and pushed it out, and then another. An ominous hum, deep, deep in the background, rose up, and resonated through her whole body. She'd been caught up with the sprint through the building, to the library, and hadn't been paying attention. She felt it now, dark, low, and dangerous.

"I feel it," said Bev.

Father Martin nodded. He walked over to a bookcase, staring at a row of books. He took a deep breath, and then slid back the glass panel, pulling out a specific book. It looked unspectacular from where Bev stood. Martin grabbed it, and slid the glass back, and then walked it over to the desk, putting it down. Bev looked at it, and it appeared normal. It looked old, but the cover wasn't leather, but normally bound, and had no writing. It was olive green, the color of books from her childhood. It wasn't even that thick, only a few inches.

"That's the book?"

"Yes," said Father Martin. He stared at it.

"Father?" Bev stared at him, and Martin didn't answer. "Hello? Father Martin?"

Bev went to him and grabbed his arm, and then he looked at her again.

"Sorry," said Martin. "It's dangerous. Even without opening it. You probably shouldn't look inside when I read."

"What?" asked Bev. "But—"

"I know," said Father Martin. "It's the thing that's inside Don, and you want to help. But frankly, it might kill me, and I don't want us both to die."

"I thought you said you knew what you were doing."

"I do," said Father Martin. "But I'm also dealing with something beyond us. And whenever that happens, pride goeth before a fall. There's always the chance of failure. We all have weak points, and artifacts like this book find them quickly, and exploit them."

"Then what should I do?"

"Watch me," said Father Martin. "If something bad starts happening, pull me away from the book. Tackle me, if you have to."

"Are you sure?"

"Yes, absolutely," said Father Martin. "But don't do it for nothing. I only have one shot at this. Are you ready?"

"I guess," said Bev. "Are you?"

He laughed. "I think so, but I guess we'll find out."

"Don't you need a notepad, or something?"

"The trouble with the knowledge contained in these books is not remembering it. It's trying to forget."

Father Martin shared one last glance with her, and then opened the book, turning the page. She stood only a few feet from him, maintaining her distance, purposefully keeping the book's contents away from her eyes. As soon as Martin began to read, he didn't break his stare away from the pages, slowly flipping them, one by one, digesting the contents, and then turning the page.

Bev watched Father Martin, his face focused, his eyes glued to the book. He sweat, even though the room was quite cool. She had no idea what was going on inside his mind, as he absorbed the information from the text. There was no movement from beyond the door. She glanced around the room, but there were only the books, and the subtle ominous hum that they produced.

Her eyes cut to Father Martin, and he still read. But as she watched him, she realized she had moved closer to him, her feet taking small steps, and then she could see the pages he looked at. She had imagined the insides of the book, and had pictured what you saw in movies. A massive tome, with yellowed paper, filled with evil diagrams and blood magic.

But the pages were just text, small, and unreadable from where she stood. She looked and found her feet moving her closer so she could read. She would need to know, just like Father Martin would need to know. If they were to defeat The Other, to cast it out of her poor husband, then she would need the information, just like he would.

Closer and closer she went, her eyes trying to decipher the information on the page, and she felt them focus hard, and her mind had sharpened to a razor point, and she was filled with cacophony, with the gnashing of teeth, with blood and claws and the screams of the dying.

Her feet still moved, and she snapped her eyes shut and forced herself backward, looking away from the book.

It almost had trapped her, still following the orders of its master, following the latent commands of The Other. Images of death and destruction had flashed through her mind in an instant, and she had tasted what Father Martin was wallowing in. She now knew why it had hurt him so much on the first experience. Why he had to steel himself to read it.

She watched, keeping her eyes only on Father Martin. The sweat beaded on his forehead, dripping down his face. He'd only been reading for under an hour, but he looked exhausted, drained. The minutes ticked by, and the pages kept flipping, almost seventy five percent through the book, only a slim number of pages remaining.

Then a thin trickle of blood slid from his nose, dripping onto his lips, down over his chin, and then off him, onto the page. But it did not stick, floating on the surface of the paper, and then he turned the page, and the blood was gone.

But more dripped from his nose, a slow trickle, and she didn't know what to do. She thought to pull him away, like he had instructed, but it was only a thin stream, and he would be done in minutes. He had only one shot, and he turned another page, even as the blood dripped from his chin. He continued to read, the nosebleed ignored.

Anxiety built inside her, and she would tackle him, and save Martin from whatever the book was doing to him. It would kill him, eating away inside him.

But then she thought to Don, and The Other, and what she would do to save him. To stop *it*.

She did nothing. The blood continued to flow.

She watched, waiting for the priest to collapse on the book, the evil doing its work on him. But he stayed upright, even as blood pooled on the desk beneath his face.

And then he was done, his hands closing the book, his eyes blinking hard, once, twice, Father Martin coming out of a fugue state, realizing himself. He wiped at his nose, his hand coming away with blood, and he reached in his pocket for a handkerchief, wiping away what he could, holding it to his face.

"I'm sorry, I didn't stop you, you were bleeding so much—"

"No, no," he said. "You did the right—" He blinked again, holding the handkerchief to his nose. "I'm—"

"Are you okay? Do you need a doctor?"

"I'll be alright," said Father Martin. "I need to rest."

"We can do that," said Bev. "Did you find the information we need? Was it in there?"

"Yes," said Father Martin, forcing the words out. "I'm sorry. It's difficult to speak. This was the right book. It has the information we need. *I* have the information we need."

"Can we stop it?"

"Yes," said Father Martin. "We can. But—" He stopped. He pulled the handkerchief away from his nose. The nosebleed had stopped.

"But what?" asked Bev.

"I'm sorry to say this, Bev," said Martin. "We can remove The Other. Banish him back to Hell, I should say. But the only way to do it is to kill Don."

27

Bev found Don sitting on the porch, looking out over their backyard. They had gotten back from his retirement party an hour ago, and she had expected to find him in bed when she got out of the shower, but he was nowhere to be found.

He glanced back at her as she pushed open the screen door. The night was cool and pleasant, and the bugs were down. He looked over the backyard, full night covering everything. He hadn't turned on the light.

"I didn't know where you were," said Bev, wearing a robe.

"Just sitting," said Don. "Didn't think I could sleep, so I thought I'd come out here and try and clear my head."

"What's wrong?" asked Bev. "I thought you were ready to leave—"

"It's not that," said Don. "Not just that. But I am ready

to leave. I taught for forty years. I think that's enough." He took a deep breath, his elbows on his knees, looking out over their yard. "I feel old, Bev."

"You're not old—"

"Yes, I am," said Don. "I'm seventy years old, Bev. If you had asked me at twenty what old was, I would have said a seventy-year-old man is *old*."

"You used to say age was just a number."

Don chuckled. "Well, I was younger. I didn't feel so god-damn ancient."

"We still have time," said Bev. "Now, we have all the time in the world. We can travel. We can sleep in. We can do whatever we want."

Don took another deep breath, and she heard something else in that breath, something ominous. She heard fear.

"Don, what's wrong?" she asked, sitting next to him, putting her hand on his shoulder.

He stared out over the land, glanced at her, and she saw the glimmer of tears in his eyes. He looked back out.

"I couldn't remember your name this morning."

"What?"

"Your name, Bev. Beverly Mills Leal. I couldn't remember your damned name, this morning."

"You know it now," said Bev. She squeezed his arm. She had noticed memory issues, of course she had, but everyone forgot things as they got older, it wasn't a big deal, it *wasn't* a big deal—

"Yes," said Don. "But how long until I forget it complete-ly?"

She hugged him then, holding him tight.

"Do you remember when we moved into this house?"

"Yeah," said Don. "It was so long ago. It seemed so big."

"Especially compared to our apartment. We thought we'd never fill it up," said Bev.

"Well, that didn't last long," said Don. "We still need to clear out some of your shoes—"

"Hey, I need those shoes."

"In case of what?" asked Don. "In case we go to fancy parties every night for the next three weeks?"

"You never know."

"Maybe with our time, we can go to a lot more fancy parties," said Don. "But somehow, I doubt we will."

"You're probably right," said Bev. "But we have plenty of time. We have a nest egg built up. We *can* travel. We can finally get this back yard squared away."

"But what if—"

"Everyone forgets things when they get older," said Bev.

"Not like this—"

"There's two of us, right?"

"Yes."

"We're a team," said Bev. "Always have been. Always will."

"I know, but—"

"If you forget something, you can lean on me," said Bev. "I'll pick up the slack."

"That's not fair to you, Bev."

"Fair has nothing to do with it, and you know it," said Bev. "When I broke my leg, and couldn't work, couldn't even cook us breakfast, what did you do?"

Don paused. "I helped pick up the slack," he said, finally.

"How long have we been married?"

"37 years," said Don. "Jeez, that's quite a while."

"You remembered that."

"How could I forget?" asked Don.

"Exactly," said Bev. "If you can't remember something, you ask me. I'll be your memory."

Don took another deep breath, and leaned over, his head on hers. "I just want all this work to be worth it. I don't want to have gotten this far, to the end of the road, and all of it to be for nothing."

"Oh, honey," said Bev. "The journey is part of it. And we took it together. And no matter how it ends, it was worth it. No matter how it ends. Okay?"

"Okay," said Don. "What are we doing tomorrow?"

"I don't know," said Bev. "I don't think we had any plans. What do you want to do?"

"I want to sleep in," said Don. "And then, I want to run to the garden center. What do you think about some flowers, over there?" He pointed.

"In the corner?" asked Bev. "We'll have to clear out all that junk back there."

"That's part of the plan," said Don. "We'll make it nice and pretty out here. Make it something we can be proud of."

"I like the sound of that," said Bev. "We've got plenty of time."

28

They returned to the US the next day. The moment they landed, and Bev turned her phone back on, she was bombarded with messages, the screen lighting up and ringing like crazy as they walked out into the terminal.

Bev hurriedly silenced it, trying to scroll through so she could listen to her voicemail. She could never get completely used to a touchscreen, she just wanted a button somewhere—

There were a dozen voicemails. The first was from the care facility. The second was from the police. She saved the rest for later.

"Don escaped the facility," said Bev. "The Other is free."

*

"Where were you, Mrs. Leal?" asked the detective. They sat in Bev's house. She had called the police back. They had sent the detective over.

"I was traveling," said Bev. "I was in Italy."

"You were in Italy? Why?" asked the detective.

"Why does it matter why I was traveling? What does that have to do with my husband's escape? Why won't you tell me what actually happened? I got off the plane, and I had a dozen voicemails, saying my husband escaped, and when I call to check in, they send someone over accosting me with questions. Where is my husband?" asked Bev. Her voice was loud, and the detective was frozen.

He paused. "We don't know, Mrs. Leal. We thought—"

"You thought that I helped him escape? I had him placed there in the first place, why the hell would I help him get out? I want him to be safe. Why won't anyone tell me what happened?"

The detective stared at her. He took a deep breath.

"Your husband murdered two employees of the care facility," said the detective. "And severely wounded five more. Three of them are still recovering in the hospital."

Bev forced back tears, a cold icepick shoved into her heart. The Other had added more misery to his tally.

"I want the details," she said.

"Mrs. Leal, I don't think—"

"I want to know," said Bev, her voice firm. "What happened?"

Another breath from the detective, as he flipped open a notepad. His tongue slipped through closed lips to wet them. "It happened three nights ago. He was locked into his room at 10 PM. At 1 AM, the nurses received a medical alert from his room, and hurried in, along with a single guard, following protocol. They found Don sitting in his chair, seemingly unresponsive. As the two nurses and the guard picked him up, to move him to the bed, he revealed a shiv and slit the guard's throat, before stabbing both of the nurses in the stomach. The guard died from his wounds within minutes. Both of the nurses survived. Are you sure you want me to continue?"

"Yes," said Bev. "Tell me."

"Don then took the billy club from the guard's body, and the keys. He locked them inside his room, and hurried to the nurse's station, where he clubbed the nurse into unconsciousness. She was the second fatality. There were two more security guards, but neither had been warned about his escape. The first was clubbed, and then handcuffed, and the second was beaten unconscious. The second guard is in a coma, and it's unclear whether they will recover. Cameras caught Don leaving the care facility at around 1:25 AM. He stole one of the guards' vehicles. It was found abandoned at a bus station the next day. We have had no leads since then."

Bev put her hands to her face. *She wouldn't cry, not anymore.* She took a deep breath, trying to calm herself down.

"I apologize for the questions ma'am, but wasn't he placed in the facility in the first place because of a car accident?" asked the detective.

"Yes," said Bev. It wasn't a lie.

"This was no accident," said the detective. "This was malicious. Callous. He brutally attacked anyone that got in his way. It was planned. It took everyone at the facility by surprise. They all claimed your husband was kind, and quiet. And then he escapes in the middle of the night, and left nothing but carnage behind. The planned nature is what concerns us. Did you have any idea at his capacity for this?"

"No," said Bev, quickly. "My husband would never do something like this. He is the kindest man I know." Still not a lie.

"There's more," said the detective. "We found a letter."

"A letter?" asked Bev.

"Yes," said the detective. "He left it behind. It was to you."

"What does it say?"

The detective reached into a pocket and pulled out a piece of paper. "The original is in with the rest of the evidence. This is a photocopy." He handed it to her. She read.

Dearest Beverly,

You can not stymie the misery by locking me away. There is no tourniquet that can stop the flow of blood. Laughing in the night as I torture Don is not enough. Your love may indeed be monumental, but it will not triumph. In fact, it will fuel my actions. I will ruin everything you have ever built. Everything that Don's name has ever touched will be burnt to the ground. When people remember you, your marriage, your husband, they will remember only the end. It will rule over it all.

Did you think that holy child could embarrass me without repercussions?

Did you think you could contain me?

This will end with fire and death.

There was no signature.

"I don't recognize this," said Bev. "This isn't from my husband. This isn't his handwriting."

"It was in his room, tucked in the shirt of the guard he killed," said the detective. "He wanted it to be found. Do you have any idea what this is referencing?"

Bev stared into the eyes of the detective and lied. "No."

He held her gaze for a second, and then nodded. "You can keep the copy. If anything comes to mind, please call us. With his diagnosis, and this behavior—we're worried he's going to hurt more people."

"I'll call if I think of anything, detective," she said. "Please, call me if you find him. And please—try not to hurt him. His mind is not what it once was."

"We'll do our best," said the detective, and then left. Father Martin came in from the dining room, where he'd been sitting on his laptop. He sat where the detective had just gotten up from.

"Did you hear all that?" asked Bev.

"Yes," said Martin. "I transcribed it all, just in case. May I see the letter?"

Bev handed it over. He read it.

"I got to him," said Father Martin.

"Yeah."

"Do you really not know what it's referring to?" asked Father Martin. "It says it will burn everything that bears Don's name to the ground. Is that just metaphor?"

"I lied," said Bev. "There's a charity that Don was active in, Math Empowering Kids. He didn't found it, but he spent hundreds and hundreds of hours building it into something. They named their center after us. The Donald and Beverly Leal Learning Center."

"That seems pretty obvious," said Father Martin. "It's a trap. He wants us to go there. He wants us to try and stop him."

"It seems like it," said Bev. "Don loved the charity, and loved helping all those kids. A lot of them went there because they found math impossible. He helped teach them it could be fun. Multiple kids went on to become math teachers themselves. He couldn't be more proud of them."

"A juicy target for The Usurper," said Father Martin. "He would have Don destroy his own legacy."

"And he wants us there."

"Well, he wants you there," said Father Martin. "He can't know if I'll still be with you. He doesn't know what we've done in the meantime."

"I—" started Bev, but she couldn't finish. "I don't know if I can stomach the cost."

"It's the only way," said Father Martin. "Believe me, I've tried to think of a loophole, but there is none."

"Are you sure?" asked Bev. "Are you sure the book has all the information?"

"Yes," said Father Martin. "That's all there is, at least for The Usurper."

"Does he know of his weakness?" asked Bev. "Does he know he can be trapped?"

"I don't know," said Father Martin. "If we disguise it well enough, I don't think he'll recognize it. But we have to plan."

"He wants us there," said Bev. "Why? Why would he tell us?"

"It feeds off misery and pain, Bev," said Father Martin. "It wants to give you a front-row seat. It probably has other plans as well. But we can trap it. We can banish it."

"I don't know—" started Bev. She looked at the walls of their home, covered in pictures of the two of them, throughout the years. Memories of their life together. Memories that shouldn't be ending, not like this. "I don't know if I can go through with this."

"If we hesitate," said Father Martin. "The Other will win, and continue his path of destruction. If you can't—well, I'll go alone."

"No," said Bev. She stared into the eyes of Father Martin. "I said I'll free him, whatever it takes."

"Then let's get ready."

29

Bev found Don's set of keys for the Math Center. They went that evening, the building quiet and closed, set back down a quiet residential street, next to a park.

"Do you think it's watching?" asked Bev, as she fumbled through the keys, finding the one that opened the building.

"I don't know," said Father Martin. "Perhaps. It wanted us here. It would wait until we arrived to strike. But the building hasn't been attacked yet."

"What if—"

"I'd worry about getting inside first, Bev," said Father Martin. "You sure we have the keys?"

"Yes," said Bev. "I'm just nervous." She tried the fifth key, and it slipped in, and turned, the lock thudding over. "There." She pushed open the door and went inside with

Father Martin. They weren't supposed to be there. They should have told the police. The authorities could have protected the building.

They'd shoot him, and The Other would escape, and there would be no peace.

They closed and locked the door behind them. It was dark inside, and Father Martin turned his flashlight on his phone, aiming through the building. It wasn't big, a few offices, a few classrooms, and one sizable meeting room, for larger events.

"Hello?" asked Bev, making sure it was empty. No answer. Better safe than sorry.

They explored the building, checking every room. No sign of anyone here, and no sign of The Other.

Beverly exhaled. She had half expected it to be waiting in the dark, jumping to attack them as they prowled through the building.

"What now?"

"We get ready," said Father Martin. He carried a shoulder bag, pulling it off and setting it on a table in the meeting room.

"What's the first step?"

"Salt," said Martin, pulling out a big box of salt from his bag, and ripping open the tab, so it could pour. He then pulled out a spray can.

"Salt?"

"Yes," said Father Martin. "Follow me." He went to the front door. He shook the can well, and then sprayed around the outside of the door, inside. Martin traced it all the way around, spraying whatever it was on thick, and then onto the floor, completing a full circuit.

"Are there any other ways into the building?"

"There's a back door," said Bev. Martin handed her the spray can. "Do what I just did to that door as well. I'll join you in a moment." Bev took the can and went to the back door, through a twisting hallway, and did the same, spraying the substance all the way around the door. Father Martin joined her a minute later, carrying the salt.

"Done?"

"Yes," said Bev.

"Good," he said, and applied the salt to the layer of the substance. "It's spray adhesive. So the salt will stick, but won't dissolve."

He laid the salt on thick, and once Bev saw what he did, she helped him finish.

"This is the first ward," said Father Martin. "If he wants inside, he has to walk through the salt."

"What does it do?"

"It's hard to explain," said Martin. "It strips away his defenses. Step by step. But the salt is just the first one."

Father Martin walked to the meeting room, the largest room in the building, back to his bag. He put the salt inside and then pulled out a small bottle.

"What's that?"

"Myrrh," said Father Martin.

"Like they gave to baby Jesus?"

"Yes," said Father Martin. "But it was a holy anointing oil. Used to bathe Christ's body. Used to *protect* Christ's body, before he resurrected."

He opened the bottle and dabbed it into a cloth he pulled from his pocket. He rubbed it around the outside of the door into the meeting room.

"The second ward," said Father Martin. "The Usurper will be trapped in the room after he crosses the threshold. He will not be able to leave."

"Are you sure about all of this?" asked Bev. "The book wouldn't lie—would it?"

"Yes, I am sure," said Father Martin. "Those books hold only truth. They are intrinsic. They hold only terrible, awful truths. I saw how to defeat The Usurper, and this is it."

"What else was in it?"

Father Martin exhaled. "It's best if I don't tell you. It's the kind of knowledge that should be contained to as few as possible." He finished rubbing the oil around the door, the outside edges gleaming with the slick oil. It smelled nice, like earth and wood. "The second ward. Be warned. He will be trapped in this room, but we will be in here with him. He will come after us. You must be prepared to defend yourself." He capped the bottle of oil and put it back in his bag, and then reached in again. She had expected another holy substance.

Instead, Martin pulled out a pistol.

"A gun?" asked Bev. He handed it to her, handle first. "What? No. I don't want that."

"Take it, Bev," said Father Martin. "I won't be able to defend us, either me or you. I'll have my hands full with the ritual. If The Other breaks free, or is too strong—you'll be defenseless. You'll have to stop it."

"But I'll just be killing Don, and it will escape," said Bev. She reached out, her hand touching the cold metal of the pistol. Father Martin pushed it into her palm. She was surprised at its weight. She'd never fired a gun before.

"This is the safety," said Father Martin. "You flip it off,

and you point it at what you want to destroy. It's loaded. You have ten shots."

"I can't—" she started, and Father Martin put his hand on her shoulder, and looked into her eyes in the dim.

"There's no other way," said Father Martin. "You have to do it. Can I trust you to pull the trigger?" He stared, and she closed her eyes, squeezing them hard, forcing the tears back.

"Yes," she said. She didn't believe her answer.

He nodded. "Help me move the tables away from the center of the room." She tucked the gun into her waist, like she'd seen in the movies, and they slid the tables to the walls. Martin went back to his bag and pulled out a dagger.

"What's that for?"

"The final ward," said Father Martin. He pulled the dagger and ran it over his palm, slicing through his skin. "Please stand back."

"Jeez," said Bev. "Don't—"

"It's the only way," said Father Martin. "The blood of a holy man. I hope I suffice." He squeezed the blood in his fist, and then dripped it onto the floor, making a square shape, scarlet soaking into the laminate floor. He winced as he pressed even more, pools of blood forming.

"You'll pass out," said Bev. "You'll—"

"No," he said. "This is it." He stopped squeezing, his hand a bloody mess, and then he got on his knees, moving the blood around on the floor, in vague shapes, painting like a toddler.

"What are you doing?"

"The final ward," said Father Martin. "In the demon's language. The language of the Abyss." Bev saw now, with the strokes of Father Martin's hand, saw the finer points, the twists and turns, the glyphs he formed.

"Don't look," said Father Martin. "It's not good for the mind."

Bev looked away, and within a few minutes, Father Martin was done. He pulled a roll of gauze from his bag and wrapped his hand, taping it down.

"You came prepared."

"We only have one chance," said Father Martin. "Let's move the tables. I want to corral him into the ward."

"Won't he see it?"

"Probably," said Father Martin. "But he believes himself invincible."

"Then why the gun?" asked Bev. "If it will succeed."

"I followed the directions to the letter, but when translating the unholy books into the real world, things can warp and change. If I believe our plan is foolproof, then we will be the ones harmed by pride. Best to plan for the worst-case scenario."

"Will your hand be okay?"

"I'll survive," said Father Martin. "If we survive tonight, I may have a scar to add to the collection."

"Well, what do we do now?" asked Bev. "If that's the final ward."

"We wait," said Father Martin. "We create ourselves a hiding spot in the dark, and we hope he comes tonight."

"What if he doesn't?"

"I think he will," said Martin. "I can—I can feel it. The Other is nearby."

They pushed tables near the far corners of the room, away from the door, and climbed underneath. Bev's hips and knees both complained as she climbed under, but it was nothing compared to the ache inside her. This was it. This was the end.

They sat in the dark, waiting, listening.

"I should tell you the complete truth, Bev," said Father Martin. "I won't have another chance."

"What do you mean?"

"I told you my father was killed by a demon," said Martin, his voice quiet in the dark.

"Yes," said Bev. "Wait, he wasn't?"

"Oh, he was," said the priest. "But it wasn't just any demon." He went silent.

"The Other," said Bev. "The Usurper."

"My father had early onset dementia," said Father Martin. "He was only forty."

"I'm sorry."

"But it shouldn't have happened so quick," said Father Martin. "The doctors didn't understand. Couldn't understand. He changed. Became evil. Dark. No one knew what was happening. But then one day, it talked to me. It taunted me. I was a little kid. No one would believe me, and that's why it told me. It laughed in my face, that same cackle. But I knew."

"What happened?"

"He killed my mother, and then himself," said Father Martin. "I was at a friend's house. It was the only reason I survived. My father—he was remembered by this terrible thing, at the end of his life. Not everything else he did. He was a good man, until then. When you told me The Usurper had taken over Don, through my door in New York—I felt like I had when I was a little kid, when it spoke to me the first time. But I knew then that I couldn't let it go free again. It can't continue this torment." He paused. "*Can* you pull the trigger, when the time comes?"

Bev felt tears come to her eyes, and she didn't stop them, this time. She let herself cry in the dark.

"This wasn't supposed to happen," said Bev. "We were going to see the world. We were going to finally do all the things we put off for years. It's not—it's not fair. I thought we had more time—" She sobbed, and then wiped her nose with her sleeve. "Can I kill my husband? Is that what you're asking?"

"Yes."

"I don't want him to die alone," said Bev. "I don't want him to die alone, trapped by that thing. Alone inside."

"I promise you, he won't die alone," said Father Martin. "However it happens, he will—"

Then there was a noise outside, and Martin went silent. The front door slammed open, and the sound of footsteps echoed into the room.

Then there was the laughter. The horrible laughter of The Other. It cackled loudly, the sound filling the building.

"Let us finish this," said The Other, his voice booming. "With fire and blood."

30

"Are you here?" asked The Other, its voice booming through the building. It vibrated through Bev's bones, shook the cement foundation below them.

"I think you are," said The Other. "I can feel you." He paused. "Ah, salt. If that is all you have, you will be very disappointed." Another pause. "Where are you? Speak up."

Bev and Father Martin hid silently, in the meeting room. The Other was outside the door, and down the hall. They didn't move. Bev forced her breathing low.

"Well, I will find you," said The Other. "I have things to do, anyway. Now is your chance to stop me, Beverly. Father." A noise reached her ears, a sloshing, splashing noise. What was he doing?

Then the smell wafted through the open door.

Gasoline.

He's going to burn down the building.

More splashing, more sloshing, and Bev pictured him walking the hall, pouring gasoline. She heard doors open, and more splashing. He was pouring it everywhere. Not missing a drop. He spoke to them as he poured.

"Will you just let me destroy his legacy, Beverly?" asked The Other. "I dug through his memories. Or at least what is left." It chuckled. "I saw so much. So much happiness. So much joy. So much charity."

Bev squeezed her hands into fists. She wanted to sprint to it, to stop it, but they couldn't. They would wait, for their trap to be sprung. It was the only way. She found Martin's eyes, gleaming in the dark. He looked at her and softly nodded.

Stay strong, his eyes said.

She nodded back.

"It burns," said The Other, his voice booming. His footsteps had tracked through the entire building. Only the big meeting room was left. "Remembering such joy. You have no idea the pain I endure. But erasing those memories. Destroying those thoughts. It is worth the pain. Because the pleasure of destruction. Of ruin, of soiling what is left of your husband's name. I cannot describe it. It is unfathomable. This building is all that remains. And I will destroy it." It paused, its footsteps stopping. "Still nothing? Are you afraid? Do you hide, cowering in the shadow?"

It walked again, splashing as it went. It was just outside the door. All Bev could smell was gasoline. Had Father Martin known? Had he realized the gasoline would mask the smell of the myrrh, of his blood?

"There are no other places to hide," said The Other, stepping into the room. Bev saw only his legs, from underneath the table. His voice was even louder now, booming.

It stopped then, both feet inside, both of Don's feet inside. It sniffed.

"Myrrh," it grumbled. "Clever. Very clever. I underestimated you, holy man."

Father Martin crawled out from underneath his hiding spot in the corner in the dim light. He stood there, on the opposite corner from The Other. Bev got out as well, following Martin's lead.

"So, you hide in here, for what?" asked The Other. "To trap me? So be it. But whatever your plan, it will not hurt me. I am invulnerable. Invincible. I am forever."

It carried a can of gas, half full. The stink of gasoline was even stronger now. Bev had to fight not to gag at the smell of it.

"You both are here. Perfect. You followed the letter." It stared at them, both. "And you did not tell the police. I knew you would not."

"Flee, demon!" commanded Father Martin. "I am a messenger of God, and I command you to leave the form of Donald Leal."

"No," said The Other.

"This is your final chance," said Martin. "I have followed the rules of etiquette."

"My final chance?" asked The Other, chuckling. "How charming. You think you have the upper hand. When mortal and infinite battle, you will always be fighting uphill."

"You are nothing," said Father Martin, calmly. "You are a child, kicking over sandcastles, that others have built. It is simple to destroy. Easy. It is hard to build. It is hard to love. You bellow, and monologue, as if what you do is difficult. Anyone can destroy a life. It's simple. It takes nothing. And yet you act like you've flipped the world over on its back." Father Martin smiled. "In all your years, you've done nothing that can even compare with the feats of Bev and Don. They built a life. They built bonds, and loved, and created something special. You think a can of gasoline compares?" Martin laughed now. "It's funny, actually. With every action, you only prove me right. You really can't escape your nature. It's sad." The Other's face darkened, his brow furrowing, his eyes full of rage.

"You dare to pity me?" bellowed The Other, stepping toward Martin, not even looking at Bev anymore. It stepped, one, two, three, four steps, and then it was inside the square, of Martin's blood, drawn into the language of Hell.

"I hold you, demon," said Father Martin, his voice hard. "Stop."

The Other froze, confusion on his face.

"What is this? What have you done?" asked The Other. He dropped the can of gas at his feet.

"I've read your book, Usurper," said Martin. And then he spoke, but what he said wasn't English. The priest's voice dropped into a gargle, a growl, and the words that came from his voice were awful, full of gnashing teeth, and pain, and cacophony. He was speaking their language. Father Martin stared at The Other now, as he spoke, first calmly, and then louder, the dark voice erupting out of Martin.

The Other stared at him with rage, unable to move.

"What are you doing?" asked The Other. "This is impossible. There is no cure for me. There is no end to me. You bind me? No. I refuse." The Other stared back, shaking, and Father Martin reacted, shaking himself. A thin trickle of blood emerged from his nose, but he didn't stop his speech.

He spoke still, engaged in this war. Bev stared, and then realized, and drew the pistol. Her palm was sweaty on the grip, rough in her hand. She put her finger to the trigger. She remembered Martin's words.

The safety. And then pull the trigger when it's pointed at something you want to destroy.

She held it, and she waited.

The two struggled, back and forth. The Other didn't speak anymore, struggling, staring, grimacing, and Bev looked at it, trying to see if Don would break through.

"Don," she said. "Please, if you're in there. Help us. Fight back. You can do it. You're stronger than it. Our love is stronger than it."

She pleaded with Don, wherever he was, and Father Martin continued to speak in the devil tongue, barking out obscene words, his voice hoarse now, but he still spoke, and The Other struggled more, shaking hard, convulsing, its teeth clacking together.

"Don, please, fight!" yelled Bev.

And then Father Martin stopped.

She looked to him, in the sudden silence. He breathed hard, blood coming from both nostrils, his eyes bloodshot, his body shaking.

The Other had frozen as well, no longer convulsing. Its eyes rolled back forward, and it was still the eyes of The Other. It looked between the two of them. Then it smiled.

Father Martin looked at her, and then she saw the blood trickle from his eyes, like tears. And then he fell, collapsing onto the ground.

The Other watched him fall. And it laughed, loud and hard, filling the room. Bev watched it, her heart cold. Father Martin laid still. He still breathed, but he was unconscious. The plan had failed. The plan had failed.

The Other stepped forward, looking at the pistol in her hand, smiling.

"What did I say?" asked The Other. "I am forever." It stepped up to her. "Did you really think that would work?"

31

"Hello, Beverly," said The Other. "Here we are. Just the two of us, once again. We stand on the cliff side. Do you want to jump?"

The Other stepped out of the final ward, the one that was supposed to bind it. Instead, Father Martin laid unconscious. She gripped the pistol hard in her hand.

It smiled, walking up to her, looking at the gun.

"Is that the fallback plan, Beverly? For you to gun me down, like Dirty Harry? Come on then. Make my day." It laughed again. "This is your chance. Your chance to cure your husband, of his unfaltering disease. One bullet. All it takes. Easy peasy. 100% success rate. Always works."

It stared at her as it advanced, getting right in her face, leering, with the eyes that weren't her husband's.

"Shoot me, Beverly," said The Other. "Shoot, and end this. Kill your husband. Do it. Shoot me."

Bev stared at The Other, rage filling her. She hated it, hated it more than she'd hated anything in her entire life, taking her husband from her, stealing their last few golden years together. Leaving her alone, without the person she'd built a life with.

She wanted to do nothing more than kill that monster, destroy that demon, and send it back to Hell. Banish it from Earth forever.

And she saw it, saw it clear as day, that this thing wasn't her husband, even if it was in his body. She raised the pistol, forcing it up, pointing at The Other's forehead.

Don's forehead.

"There you go," said The Other. "You can do it, darling."

"You shut your mouth," said Bev. "You go to Hell."

"But I will not, Beverly," said The Other, smiling, talking in that dark voice. "I will flee, and inhabit another form, far from here. You will never see me again. Unless you watch the news closely. And then maybe you *will* see me, when another innocent takes more lives. When another person destroys their legacy. You will have to look closely, though. But it will be the end of *your* suffering. Of your husband's. But I will continue. I will persist."

It stood still, holding its head steady for her aim. She pressed the barrel of the gun to its skin—*Don's skin*—and she flicked off the safety, her finger on the trigger.

"Almost there," said The Other. "One more step. Pull the trigger."

She held the pistol, feeling the tension on the trigger with her finger. Bev held it there, on the edge, her heart aching.

She dropped the pistol beside her. She couldn't do it. Bev couldn't do it, no matter how much she hated The Other. She loved Don too much.

The Other laughed loudly, again, uproariously, and it rang in her ears, and then it grabbed her wrist, and pulled her back to the center of the room. She couldn't resist its strength, its impossible strength, and it pulled her right into the final ward, the final ward which had only stopped it momentarily. It pulled her in and danced with her over the blood of the priest. Father Martin still laid there, his chest slowly moving.

It dragged her through the movements, and she couldn't resist, there was no more resistance in her. She couldn't stop it, there was nothing she could do but shoot it, and give it exactly what it wanted. It wanted her to fire, to kill Don, and give it the chance to flee into another body. Leaving her with nothing but the murder of her husband.

"So be it, Beverly," said The Other. "So be it. Let's see how far we can go, then." It danced with her, and kicked over the gas can, the rest of the liquid spilling out onto the floor, over the blood of Father Martin. It stank, the room filled with the gas vapor. "Kill me now, Beverly, before I destroy what is left of your husband's name. Stop me, if you can." It dropped her, letting her fall, and then fished into a pocket, pulling out a lighter. It flicked it once, twice, and a small flame emerged.

Bev felt tears cover her face, and realized she'd been crying this entire time, and she should shoot it, she knew, but she couldn't raise her hand. It was right to burn this all down. They would die together.

"Still nothing?" asked The Other. "Oh, well." It threw

the lighter into the pile of gas, and it lit immediately into a pyre with a *whoosh*. The heat washed over her, and the flames spread, to the tables, chairs, and floor. He grabbed her again, pulling her to her feet, pulling her tight in an embrace. Being that close to The Other made her stomach roil, and she swallowed back bile. It smiled in her face, and she smelt its breath, different from Don's smell. There was nothing this demon didn't touch with its possession.

"This is the end, Beverly," it said in her ear. "Here we are. A front-row seat. I could not have imagined a better scenario. I want to thank you for coming this far. People usually give up much sooner." The flamed licked even higher up the walls, swirling around them. They soon blocked the door. The inferno trapped them. The heat was oppressive, and the smoke was high. She was finding it hard to breathe.

"Unfortunately, this will be the end of our relationship. I will leave you here, with your husband. Enjoy your final moments. It is time for me to bid my adieu." Then The Other's eyes rolled back, and she expected him to go. At least she would have Don here, at the end. Father Martin hadn't lied. He wouldn't die alone.

But then The Other's eyes came back. He was still there. He let her go, dropping her to the floor. The air was better there, and she could breathe again.

Rage and confusion filled The Other's face.

"What did you do?" asked The Other. Its eyes moved again, but returned. "I cannot leave. No! This is impossible. I am infinite. I persist!"

Bev looked up at the demon and smiled at it for the first time. She narrowed her eyes.

"Is that right?" she asked.

"No! I refuse!" it bellowed. "I will not allow it!"

"I don't think you have much of a choice anymore," said Bev. She felt the gun in her hand. It felt lighter.

"No, no, no! I am in control! I will not allow this, I am powerful, I am forever, you cannot restrain me, a mortal cannot—"

The Other shook, much like it had when Father Martin recited the words of its language. Its eyes rolled back once again.

When they opened, it was Don in control. He smiled.

"Don?" asked Bev. "I thought—"

Don dropped next to her, hugging her, squeezing her as tight as he could. But only with love.

"I've been biding my time, darling," he said. "It takes a lot to push it back down. But I figure now's as good a time as any. It's still in me, but I've got him tied down, for a moment."

"Oh, Don," she said, squeezing even tighter. She held him back and kissed him hard on the mouth, as hard as she'd ever kissed him. She pulled back, and looked into his gentle eyes. "I'm sorry."

"Oh, it's not your fault," he said. "You've done everything you could. Some things—well, some things we can't control."

"We were supposed to have more time," said Bev. "We were going to do so much more."

"We were, that's true," he said. "But how many years did we get?"

"A good number," she said. "A lifetime's worth."

"And no matter how it ends, how ugly it gets here at the end, it doesn't change any of those memories. You'll still have them. And when you need me, that's where I'll be."

A sudden noise shocked Bev, from above them. Suddenly, the sprinkler system kicked on. Water rained down on them. The flames died down within moments.

Don smiled. "I managed to keep some information from it." Bev laughed, despite it all. She stared into his eyes.

"I don't want to lose you," said Bev.

"Oh, darling," he said. "You were going to lose me, anyway. This bastard just sped things up a little. I can feel it. It's struggling, mightily. It doesn't like this joy we're getting. I can feel it pushing back up."

"So this is it?" she asked, tears flowing down her face.

"It is, for now," said Don. "Whatever's waiting after this—well, I'll be on the lookout for you. Give me the high sign, and I'll find you."

"I love you," said Bev. "I love you, and I always will."

"I love you, too," said Don. "Goodbye, darling."

"Goodbye," said Bev.

"I'm going to let The Other back up," said Don. "As soon as you see his eyes, you kill that son of a bitch." She nodded, and then his eyes closed. She raised the pistol to his head, at arm's length.

When they opened again, they were The Other.

"Burn in Hell," she said, and fired.

32

The hospital was quiet in the middle of the day. Machines beeped distantly, and Bev heard hushed conversations on the phone in the background, but it all washed over her.

The chair wasn't comfortable, not really. She hoped Father Martin would be free soon. She felt exposed out here, in the row of plastic chairs in the hospital corridor.

It had been two weeks since they'd banished The Other, and since she'd killed Don.

There had been no funeral, and no service, not yet. Don had been cremated as soon as the police had released his body. It was what he wanted, what they both wanted. He had wanted to be cremated, and his ashes spread.

His urn sat in the house. She hadn't spread his ashes yet, couldn't, not yet. Something pulled at her.

And it wasn't just the news about Don's death. That had been the reason for delaying the memorial service.

The people killed at the farmer's market, and the people dead in the care facility. Honoring Don's life, when those poor people were just being buried themselves.

It wasn't Don that killed them, Bev knew that, but still, those people deserved what little peace they could get. If delaying Don's service helped them in even a small way, that's what she would do. Maybe a year from now, they would have something, something modest, and it would let everyone grieve. She didn't need the service, not really, not after—

The door to Father Martin's room opened, and two older priests walked out, both looking tired. They both briefly made eye contact with her, and nodded solemnly, but neither had spoken with her, and neither spoke with her now, leaving quietly.

Bev pushed herself out of the uncomfortable plastic chair and into Martin's room. He laid on the bed, the adjustable mattress propped up so that he half sat. He'd been laid up ever since that night at the learning center. For the first few days, he'd been unable to speak. The doctors had diagnosed it as a stroke, or a severe concussion. None of the scans proved conclusive, but Bev hadn't expected the doctors to recognize what battle with a demon did to someone's mind or flesh. The scans had never found evidence of The Other inside Don, either.

Bev closed the door quietly and sat in the chair closest to the bed.

"How are you feeling?" asked Bev.

"Better, now that those two dinosaurs are gone," said Father Martin. He smiled.

"What did you talk about?"

"About The Other. About Don, and you."

"What did you tell them?"

"I told them that we had failed you," said Martin. "And that the Church must do better in the future about demons that walk among us. That despite the fact that The Other is gone, there are still more, and we must be vigilant. We must study." Martin took a deep breath. "I don't think they listened."

"But we have evidence," said Bev. "Smoke inhalation didn't give you a concussion. Don's sudden change in behavior, the murders, the note he left—it doesn't take Sherlock Holmes to notice the trend."

"They were sensitive to your loss, and to my injuries," said Father Martin. "But I doubt they'll push for any change." He paused. "I will, though, as soon as I'm feeling better. That might be a while. My mind—it's still foggy. A little slow. I'm beginning to believe that the demon took some years off my life."

A silence fell between them, and Bev looked at Father Martin's face. He looked exhausted, and his eyes lagged a little, slower than they were before.

"Is it really gone?" asked Bev. "The Other?"

"Yes, I think so," said Martin. "You said it yourself. It was there. We were trapped. It tried to leave, and couldn't. The wards worked as they should have. You succeeded where I failed—"

"We wouldn't have made it that far without you—"

"You pulled the trigger, Bev. The hardest part. Have the police—" started Martin, but trailed off.

"Bothered me anymore?" asked Bev. "No. They believed me. Like I said, we have evidence. We had the note. His fingerprints were on the gas can. Don had lost his mind at the end of his life, and we did what we had to."

"It's not entirely false," said Father Martin. "But it was best not to mention the demon. It would only complicate matters."

Bev took a deep breath. "I still worry—"

"Worry?" asked Father Martin, eyeing her. "That The Other will come back?"

"Yes," said Bev. "I've been having trouble sleeping. I keep expecting a stranger to knock on my front door. Possessed by that bastard, coming back for revenge."

Father Martin met her eyes. "We still have a lot to learn about Hell, and the creatures that inhabit it, but they can't cross over unbidden. Someone summoned The Usurper, many years ago, in a fit of hubris, and it would require someone else to summon it again. The only book that has that information is locked in the Vatican's library, where we read it. It is safe there."

"Is it?" asked Bev. "We got to it."

"Even the most corrupt priest would know to not tamper with those books," said Father Martin. "And if there is one—well, The Other would be the least of our worries." He looked at her. "We are safe from it, Bev. It is gone. I am sorry that it also cost Don."

"I got to say goodbye," said Bev. A tear snaked down her cheek, and she wiped it away. "It's more than what some people get. And we kept that monster from hurting anyone else."

"Another lasting legacy of Don's," said Father Martin.

"Your love won out."

*

The house was quiet.

Bev was tempted to leave the television on, like they typically did, but she resisted the urge. It would fill the house with noise, and distract her, and even make her feel like she wasn't alone.

But she was alone. And she wouldn't have her grief and loneliness be tempered.

The chaos, menace, and threat of The Other had been replaced by peace. Bev slept now, deep, and long sleep, sleep that threatened to take her day away, because sleep was a blessed reprieve from her grief.

But she would not let sleep temper her grief either, and she forced herself awake, into habits and routines. Occasionally, her eye would catch Don's urn, sitting on their mantel. He had wanted his ashes spread, and there was no time like the present, but Bev kept walking past them. He wanted her to do it, and her alone. But—

But nothing, Beverly. The past few months changed nothing, and you know it.

Bev sat down on the couch and looked up at Don's urn.

"It's different now," she said. "You know that. Would you still want them in the same place? After everything we went through?"

The urn didn't answer.

"We didn't have time to discuss it," said Bev. "It was the last thing on my mind. I was worried about The Other. I was worried about—you."

She stared at the urn.

"Alright," she said. "Alright. I know, I know. I know what you would have wanted. I know you wouldn't want The Other to affect how we behaved, how I behaved. It would be letting it win, and we beat that son of a bitch."

Bev took a deep breath. She felt tears well in the corner of her eyes.

"I don't want to go out there," said Bev. "I remember—"

She stopped.

"Yeah, I know," said Bev. She looked at the urn again. "I know." She got up, walking to the urn, and grabbing it from the mantel. "I should go now, when the sun is bright." Bev slipped on her yard shoes and went out the back door. She didn't bother locking it. The sun shone high in the sky. She held Don in her arms, cradling his ashes like a baby.

Bev walked through the backyard, and out the back gate, tracing steps she'd made a thousand times. Most recently, following The Other, as he led Don out into the forest, to the cliff.

To frighten her.

To hide a terrible crime.

Now darling, don't think like that.

He was right.

She didn't think of the harrowing journeys into the forest.

She thought of the many journeys before that. Of quiet strolls. Of peace, and conversation, and walks that led to the cliff, and of the two of them together, enjoying the sun streaming through the trees.

How many were there?

Too many to count. They had walked this path many,

many times. The good outnumbered the bad, many times over. She thought of them.

When they had first moved in.

When they got promotions.

When they needed to think.

When they needed to retreat.

And love ruled over all those instances.

Bev took step after step, walking the familiar path through the forest on the gentle incline, her breath coming harder now. She took the same steps she did when she was ten, twenty, and thirty years younger. And in those younger days, Don walked with her.

She carried him today.

But not much longer.

The cliff was where it always was, the bench a few feet back from the edge, the sun out, pouring through the canopy. The cliff fell in front of her.

Where The Other had threatened her, and Don.

But also where they had sat together. Where they had embraced.

Bev could have said a thousand words, a lifetime of love and appreciation and everything, but instead, she opened the urn, and gently poured the ashes over the edge. Don's ashes caught on the breeze, and slowly floated down, settling in the forest.

It was what he wanted. To be nearby. She could visit him anytime.

Bev waited, letting Don fall out of sight.

She sat down on the bench, putting the now empty urn next to her. Her life waited for her, back at the house.

It could wait a few minutes.

SIGN UP FOR TWO FREE, EXCLUSIVE NOVELS!

Sign up for Robbie's newsletter! Monthly sneak peeks at upcoming projects, cover teases, and instant access to TWO FREE, EXCLUSIVE novels!

www.robbiedorman.com/newsletter

About the Author

Robbie Dorman believes in horror. The Other is his twelfth novel. When not writing, he's podcasting, playing video games, or petting cats. He lives in Texas with his wife, Kim.

You can follow Robbie on Twitter @robbiedorman

ACKNOWLEDGEMENTS

Thank you to my wife Kim, for her patience and support. Thank you to my team of beta readers; Andrew, Matt, Megan, and Yousef, for your guidance and help. Thank you, for reading.

9 781958 768013